BARBARA HANRAHAN

WHERE THE QUEENS
ALL STRAYED

ABOUT *UNTAPPED*

Most Australian books ever written have fallen out of print and become unavailable for purchase or loan from libraries. This includes important local and national histories, biographies and memoirs, beloved children's titles, and even winners of glittering literary prizes such as the Miles Franklin Literary Award.

Supported by funding from state and territory libraries, philanthropists and the Australian Research Council, *Untapped* is identifying Australia's culturally important lost books, digitising them, and promoting them to new generations of readers. As well as providing access to lost books and a new source of revenue for their writers, the *Untapped* collaboration is supporting new research into the economic value of authors' reversion rights and book promotion by libraries, and the relationship between library lending and digital book sales. The results will feed into public policy discussions about how we can better support Australian authors, readers and culture.

See untapped.org.au for more information, including a full list of project partners and rediscovered books.

Readers are reminded that these books are products of their time. Some may contain language or reflect views that might now be found offensive or inappropriate.

To Jo Steele

Have you ever been down to my countree?
  it was full of smiling queens:
They had flaxen hair, they were white and fair,
  but they never reached their teens.
Their shoes were small and their dreams were tall:
  wonderful frocks were worn;
But the queens all strayed from the place we played
  in the land where I was born.

John Shaw Neilson

I

We hadn't always lived at Fern Gully. Once there'd been a house at Prospect, by the hotel. Father had been a tram driver. He'd come home with his kit-bag, whistling every night; the smell of beer wasn't melancholy then. He'd been different—smiling a lot; he didn't spend the day with the sad look on his face. Even his beard seemed curlier. But the house at Prospect was before the accident. Father hadn't been lame when a tram in the distance meant you might see him—a hero as good as Uncle Will.

One day they'd carried him home and there was blood on his great-coat and Doctor said he might lose the leg. Mother started to cry, and Meg and I were afraid. She'd never cried so much before. Not even when the news came that Uncle had died in South Africa. But Father's leg going lame made Mother strong. She'd dried her eyes and taken charge. The house at Prospect was sold, and Mother's past began to merge with the present.

We climbed on top of a Hill & Co. coach and drove past the market-gardens and orangeries of Payneham and Athelstone. Meg and I perched beside the driver on his box. It was lovely being up so high, swinging along, the horses' hoofs beating out a message. There was so much to see. We drove along the banks of the Torrens, and one of Mother's best stories was all about that. "Once," it began, "the river had a better name. The Aborigines called it Karra Wirra Pari, which means River of the Red Gum Forest ..."

We drove into the Hills. There were gum-trees and, at intervals, houses. Ladies in their gardens stopped hanging out washing and shaking the crumbs from tablecloths to wave. The driver jiggled his reins, and looked proud as he told us that the passing of the coach was the great event of the ladies' days.

"Good gracious," they'd say, "there's the coach, and the fire not
alight", or "Pussy not fed", or "the kettle not on the boil".

The road kept zigzagging. There were sharp rises and steep
descents. I clung to Meg and worried that the driver might lose
a rein, and the horses bolt. One dangerous declivity was known
as Breakneck Cutting.

Soon the country changed. It was gentler, almost English.
There were paddocks and orchards and farms. Mother's eyes
shone. Though Father disregarded the view, and concentrated
on his leg as if he felt a pain, she ignored him. She looked about
her and smiled. She had grown up in the Hills; she loved them.

So often Mother told stories of the pioneers. How they'd
come to a new country, and everything was strange. To feel safe
they'd thought of home. The kangaroo grass might have been
corn; the Adelaide plains, nicely wooded, resembled a gentleman's park. They missed the old things so much that they sent
to India for slips of apple- and pear-tree. Granma had come to
South Australia with a root of rhubarb wrapped in moss. She
placed it in a box with her shoes, the leather of which kept it
moist.

Mother had been a pioneer at Prospect. She was permanently homesick. Instead of transplanting rhubarb, she'd summoned up the Hills with words.

She said they were more like England than any other place
in the state. As well as tea-tree and wattle there were ivy bushes
and oak-trees, hedges of sweet-brier and monthly roses. The
highest and most central point in the Hills was Mount Lofty.
The Mount was Elysium. Up there were ribbon gardening and
marble statues and the dwellings of fashionable society. Each
mansion was surrounded by plants that would have died on the
plains in summer. There were rhododendrons, camellias, even
strawberries. In winter it was known for snow to fall.

The horses made spanking time, and soon we came to Fern
Gully. Its name was something of a misnomer. The town did
not lie in the gully, but on its adjacent slopes. Whatever may

have been the case formerly, fern was not conspicuous among its vegetation.

The first thing that arrested attention was a patriotic memorial close to the Post Office. On it was Uncle Will's name. In Fern Gully, Uncle was famous. As Trooper William Jones of the Australian Bushmen's Corps he'd died in action against De Wet's guerrilla forces in South Africa. His horse and he were felled by the same bullet; but only Uncle was a hero, entitled to that sturdy pebble-dash obelisk.

Mother leaned forward to point out the different churches. The Baptist with the field below it where stood a circle of fourteen oak-trees, the Methodist with its imposing manse, the Anglican that boasted a baptismal font made from best English Bath-stone. There were shops and little houses with names like the houses had at Prospect: Globe Villa, The Wattles.

Then it was time to climb down, for the coach had stopped. We had reached the lane where Granma lived. My legs were trembly from sitting so long; I wanted to go to the lavatory. I felt sad as the driver waved goodbye, for he'd turned into a friend.

Our luggage had been sent on ahead, so there was only Mother's basket to carry. Father and Meg shared its handles. I held Mother's hand and had to run to keep up, she set off down the lane at such a pace.

I began to feel excited again. The lane was part of the adventure, part of Mother's past. Walking down it was like walking into a series of her stories.

There were the remains of the oldest wattle and daub hut in the district. Once a gentleman lived there who'd lost one of his hands in a winnower, and wore a metal stump into which he screwed a hook for use when gardening, and a dinner fork for service when at meals. He was a dedicated gardener: Mother recalled the hook as having a high degree of polish.

Even the trees were old friends. The blue gum twined with mistletoe; the red gum that was the home of laughing jacks and rosella parrots. We passed the patch of stringybarks where

you found Dutch orchids, and the prickly acacias where Jenny
Wren built her nest.

We came to the shiny green hedge that was called the
squeaker hedge, because its leaves did for a whistle if you folded them in halves and blew hard. Beyond the hedge was Lizzie
Potter's house. It was as curious as I remembered from the last
time we'd visited Granma: made of silvery tin that shone in the
sun, and set about with sunflowers and cockleshell borders. I'd
never seen it, but I knew there was a grape-vine at the back of
the house with a stem as thick as a lady's waist. Though best of
all, apparently, was Lizzie herself. I took Mother's word for it
that she rivalled any fairy-tale witch.

We halted beside another hedge—this time of shrubby
wormwood. And now Mother seemed to have strayed into one
of the stories, too. She had a part to play that was nothing to do
with Father and Meg and me. We might have been no relation.
She shook free of my hand and ran ahead of us towards a house
shaded by creepers and a corrugated-iron verandah. Under the
verandah stood a fat lady, dressed in black because of Uncle
Will.

And then it was funny, for it appeared Mother had made
a mistake; had run into the wrong story, muddled another's
childhood with her own. When she reached the verandah the
fat lady dodged her arms. Mother ended up hugging bridesmaid's fern and morning glory.

Gran loved us, Mother assured, but I found it hard to believe.
All the way to Fern Gully on the coach, and walking along the
lane, I'd imagined us coming nearer to nicely bestowing a favour. Our arrival would be just the thing to cheer an old lady's
lonely days. It was always like that in the books Meg got for
Sunday School prizes. It had been something like that when
we'd visited Granma twice a year. She'd let me look in the box
that was full of mementoes of Uncle. I saw the silver leaf he'd
sent from Table Mountain, the indelible pencil scored by his

teeth. I was Gran's favourite, because my name—Thea—was short for Dorothy, which was hers. She cut me a second slice of marble cake, and the goodbye kiss I received was wetter than Meg's. She played at perfect grandmother as she sent us back to Prospect laden with eggs and honey and rhubarb.

When you saw her every day she was different. Everything else was, too. The eggs didn't taste so good when you had to collect them in the morning before school, yourself ... in winter it was cold; always, you were scared of the spiteful hen that pecked. And bees stung, and though the story of the rhubarb's coming was romantic, Meg said she saw a black snake by the patch. Cross her heart—though Granma swore at her and said she was a city-bred fool.

Old ladies weren't meant to swear, but Granma did. She said bloody cow and bugger and took God's name in vain. Mother looked nervous when one of the temper fits was coming. Father could disappear to have a smoke behind the fowl-house, but not she.

Perhaps the most disconcerting thing was that Mother kept telling her stories. Even after Granma snipped the buttons from Meg's new Dorothy bolero she could tuck me into bed and tell of a gentle Gran in bias-cut flounces ... they ran up her skirt from hem to waist, so that when she walked she rippled. Mother swore the story to be true, but I didn't believe her. Granma could never have been like that. She could never have made a jelly with a lot of isinglass and a little water, then rode in a buggy with it wrapped in wet cloth, on her lap ... for the party was thirty miles away and there was no ice.

I scorned Mother's stories as much as I hated Gran. Both of the actions hurt. Though they'd both betrayed me—one by lying, the other by loving falsely—I felt that if I kept scorning, yet went on savouring the stories and enjoying the marble cake that was still a part of tea-time, I somehow did the betraying myself. Though, with regard to Granma, there was more than merely cake to savour. She didn't have the fits all the time. In between, she could be all right. I helped her peel the potatoes, and she showed me how you saved the skins cut thick at the eyes for planting. Together we spread the wet sheets on top of the scented bushes in the garden to dry.

Doing those things it was easy to believe she'd been young and pretty and nice. Sometimes when she was like that, her eyes looked bewildered. I waited in vain for her mouth to come open and tell the secret: why there was another Granma who was different.

Perhaps she was mad; perhaps it was something to do with Uncle Will's dying, and that of Granpa before him. Or being lonely for too long before we came, or realizing that you could even die yourself. All the time we lived with her, Gran was two people. Really, I both loved and hated her. It would have been easier if she'd been nasty all the time. I wondered why I cried myself to sleep.

One morning after a particularly bad fit the night before—she'd smashed Mother's crystal scent bottle, and set fire to the fringes of the rug—we found her dead in bed. It hadn't been a peaceful dying. Granma's contorted face showed she'd even tussled with Death.

I missed her, but things improved. Gran lay in the cemetery by the Recreation Ground, and Mother's stories came into their own. There was no longer any awkward reality to mock the fabled pioneer lady who carried a jelly on her lap, and had a rhubarb root sprouting from her shoe.

The Hills became home. The years passed, and it seemed a dream that we'd ever lived at Prospect, where Father had whistled and woken regularly with a smile on his face. For though she was under the earth, and in winter hemmed in by an extra layer of nettles and grass, a little of Granma's power lingered on. When she'd been taken with one of the tempers she'd usually vented her rage on Father. "He's not good enough," she'd cry. "They only lived at Bowden, by the gasworks." And she said he drank like a fish, that he'd a hide as thick as a rhino's. She said he was living off her money—wrapping apples, now and then, didn't count. Why hadn't he been man enough to get killed in South Africa like Will? "Bugger his leg," she'd say when Mother tried to defend him.

I knew what she said wasn't true. Bowden didn't matter ... but it did. There *was* a gasworks; there was a boot factory and a tannery and a bottle works, too. Bowden was common. Father gave Meg the book of sacred solos that had been his mother's, and she got rid of the horrid address: "Fourth Street, Bowden" with fierce black strokes of her pen.

And he sensed all the nasty secret untrue things we judged him with. And each year he became quieter. What Meg did hurt the most. Everyone knew he loved her best.

2

Once Meg had been merely my older sister; someone familiar, whom I took for granted. She was nice enough, but ordinary; I didn't notice her much. Then one day I was twelve and she was seventeen. She put her hair up, and I looked at her properly, and found I didn't know her. Overnight, it seemed, she'd turned into a stranger who did all the things the Ladies' Page of the *Observer* advised: whitened her neck with a cut lemon dipped in toilet borax, rubbed in dainty Russian skin food every night. Hands were the great test of breeding, so she wore a pair of gloves to bed. She read novels called *The Gaiety of Fatma* and *A Gamble With Life*. She knew the masculine Gibson Girl to be out of fashion; that the "restful" type was the girl of today.

Because of Meg our life changed. She made Mother buy Cashmere Bouquet soap instead of Pears, for the ad vowed Madame Bernhardt said it was exquisite, *par excellence* the toilet soap of the refined. All sorts of things became as common as Bowden. Father had to change his tobacco from Yankee Doodle to Irish Civil; the sauce bottle wasn't allowed on the table.

She demanded an underskirt festooned with real Torchon lace, and a bead necklet from the Feather Shop in Melbourne. She debated should it be lessons at the Adelaide Shorthand and Business Training Academy, or the School of Design on North Terrace. She decided on the latter as being more genteel. Twice a week she took the morning coach in, to study repoussé work and artistic anatomy. She started to talk silly. She said things about the thrush's liquid melody and the perfume of the golden wattle. The apple blossom down by the jam factory made her feel choky. When the choir sang "Out on the Rocks" at morning service she had tears in her eyes.

Probably the tears had something to do with Teddy Teakle; likewise feeling choky, when confronted by Teakle apple-trees.

One day Teddy would own those trees, and acres of others as well. The jam factory would be his, too. No wonder Meg's eyes were liquid in church. She looked better than ever like that, and she knew Teddy was watching, swivelling his head in the Teakle pew across the aisle. When it was time for a hymn, she sang with ardour and poppy cheeks, holding her head high to show off the dimple in her chin and give her nose a chance of more tilt. It was all right to flirt—as long as you did it ladylike, and kept on singing for Jesus.

Teddy's father talked a lot of his old Welsh mother who'd walked miles to the fair with a box of eggs on her head and a poultry basket on her arm, the while knitting a pair of stockings. He boasted of being a self-made man, who'd started off poor in the wood-carting business, and by dint of great energy and toil had purchased land at Fern Gully. He'd cleared it bit by bit, planting it first with trees that eventually bore the Cleopatras, Rome Beautys, and Jonathans he'd taken a chance on exporting to England. The apples paved the way for the plums and cherries and apricots that led on to the jam factory, and the familiar Teakle tin banded with Great Exhibition medals that graced self-respecting larders throughout the state.

But though Mr Teakle was a man of the people, he took care to see his only son stayed unrelated. Mrs Teakle, who'd come from modest Gully stock herself, had obligingly died giving birth. Teddy had been sent off early to a boarding school in the city.

He grew up to be a figure of romance. The jam factory was down in a hollow. When it was summer and school holidays came, the Gully Road was a favourite route for girls of initiative out on a ramble. In the old days, when Meg was still ordinary and not playing at proper young lady, we'd take a turn there ourselves to be entertained.

I thought the girls beautiful, coming towards us from town

like a troupe of angels, all in their best, all in white—white dresses, hats, and sunshades—set off nicely by the trees so green and
the sky so blue. When they came to Teakle's they bent over the
hedge at the side of the road, pretending to look for roses; or
someone was sure to discover a pebble in her shoe, or someone
else to complain of stitch. You could tell by their giggles or sighs
if they'd sighted him or not. Usually they hadn't. Their shoulders drooped as they went back to town.

Though, as we passed them, I saw the damp patches under
their arms and smelled that their scent was only cheap, they
stayed beautiful in my imagination. They were as much a part
of the romance as Teddy.

One day we were lucky enough to sight him ourselves. Meg
saw a hole in the hedge and we pushed through it and ran between trees. We squatted behind a tangle of blackberries. Beside the factory was a house and, as we watched, the front door
opened and Teddy appeared. His hair was black and shiny, like
that of a ventriloquist's doll; his skin was as pale as egg white.

After that, we tried to find out all about him. Meg read in the
Observer of the Young People's Dance, very fashionable, held at
the school. His name leapt from a list of anonymous others. It
was thrilling to hear how dancing had taken place in the Assembly Hall hung with palm leaves and bunting. But Meg stopped
reading when she came to the bit about the desks carved with
names famous in the history of school and state that had served
as resting places for various dainty cloth coats edged with fur.

Teddy left school, and then it was better than ever. Hardly
a week went by that we didn't read his name. He was at the
Town Hall to hear Madame Dolores render "I Know That My
Redeemer Liveth" in excellent voice; there were euchre parties,
and a trip to Port Victor *en automobile*.

Teddy only led a quieter life when he became a student at
the School of Design, dedicating himself to Beauty's flaming
torch. He turned into an artist, highly accomplished. The Art
Gallery purchased a still life picture from his brush.

He went on living in the house beside the jam factory. His father had a studio built on at the back and he called his bedroom a den. It was rumoured to be decadent, almost like a lady's boudoir. Instead of the pipe-racks you'd expect, silverpoint decorated the walls. Embroidered hangings took the place of boxing gloves and antlers. Flowers abounded; there was a brazier for burning aromatic woods.

Meg and Teddy were soul-mates. She did repoussé and artistic anatomy; he kept up his painting. You'd come across him here and there at vantage points about the Gully, poised on a collapsible stool, all the while looking beautiful. He wore a corduroy suit even when it was a heat-wave.

I was sure Meg was meant to marry him. I had the details of where they'd live planned already. I fancied Glenelg, because that meant the seaside, and the famous old gum-tree under which the colony had been proclaimed; and it was a lucky name, staying the same, even when spelled back to front. It would be nice to visit them a lot, to go for paddles and then brush the sand from your hair and catch the train to the city … it would be an adventure, with everything new, yet it would only be a holiday, I wouldn't have to say goodbye to the Hills. I allowed them a Queen Anne house roofed with Marseilles tiles. There'd be a sufficiency of gables and spires, each topped with something patriotic—a fretwork emu, or, best of all, dear old kanga on a gum-nut speckled stump. The verandah would drip cast-iron as frilly as an afternoon-tea doilie's edging. Inside there'd be a patent gas cooker, an ice-box …

There was only one thing wrong. So far the principals in my love-match hadn't spoken.

For Mr Teakle had his eye on something more exotic than a Gully girl for Teddy. And while his father's hand was on the purse-strings Teddy stayed obedient. He was content to adore from an aisle away; he allowed himself only Sunday glances.

3

The lane became as much mine as Mother's. I loved every part of it: the gum-trees and sugar-ants, the wattle and daub hut. Even its patches of weeds were precious; I cared as much for soursobs and Salvation Jane as I did for monthly roses. I was always running up and down it. The place I liked going to most was Lizzie Potter's house of tin. Familiarity couldn't diminish its fairy-tale aspect. It shone so silver in the sun that you had to screw up your eyes to look. Here and there on the tin were shadowy traces of trademarks: St George and the dragon, a royal crown.

The inside of the house didn't disappoint, either, for Lizzie liked to collect things.

New things didn't interest her. To be worthy of Lizzie's collection an object had to be old, second-hand, flawed. She treasured what others abandoned. She frequented the rubbish dump by the creek.

Sometimes I went there with her. I helped push the basket-work perambulator Lizzie put her finds in.

Walking beside her, I saw things differently. Newspapers and rusting tins seemed scattered for decoration. They complemented the landscape; they did for Chinese lanterns and bunting. When the wind blew, a sheet of corrugated iron made a sound as good as a harp.

We were off on an eccentric paper-chase. I walked through the bush with my head down, concentrating on the little world at my feet. Together we made discoveries that matched any history-book explorer's. It was Lizzie who first showed me the lily called lady's finger; who made me sniff the fragrant bark of the sandalwood-tree that others called native myrtle. When the perambulator came to a halt, and she stooped over some new treasure—a mildewed almanac, a teapot without a handle—I was free to gather rattlepods and old man's gold.

Sometimes we were lucky and came upon a courting couple. Lizzie cautioned me to be quiet, but she had no need. I was proud of the way I almost stopped breathing as we strained forward to catch a glimpse of lovesick flesh.

Lizzie had spent years perfecting her peeping. She'd kept an eye on generations of Gully couples up to tricks. What she didn't know about skeletons in the cupboard didn't count. But she wasn't disliked. She was too kind for that.

She brought back clothes from the dump. What she didn't want herself, she'd cut up and sew into something useful—maybe a pinafore for a child. She'd trim it with braid and say: "Here's your Christmas present." If it was something knitted she found, she'd spend ages unpicking it. "Here's a ball of wool for you," she'd say. "Wool's expensive, you know."

Lizzie knew all sorts of remedies for sickness. She filled the perambulator with herbs and leaves and roots. Nettles were good for the blood; dock was an ingredient in poultices. Honeysuckle flowers and eucalyptus leaves yielded syrup for sore throats and colds. Wattle bark could be made into a soothing lotion for unbroken burns and scalds.

All these things found their way into Lizzie's kitchen, to simmer in a cauldron or soak in a three-legged pot. Brewing her medicines, Lizzie looked more like a witch than ever. She stirred with the copper-stick; her face dissolved and reappeared through a shifting spiral of fumes.

I could never decide if she was beautiful or ugly. With people like Teddy and Meg you knew right away, and went on to take their looks for granted. Lizzie stayed a problem.

From being out in all weathers her face was tanned. There were the wrinkles—sun-rays about the eyes, grooves on her forehead, more rays about the mouth from smiling. I never knew if she had any hair, for she always wore a cabbage-leaf

hat. Under her clothes she might have been thin. There were so
many layers, each smelling of medicine flavourings and sweat.
Beneath a high-buttoned coat were indications of a variety of
costumes: a red flannel jacket, moleskin trousers, a Rob-Roy
plaid skirt.

Summer turned the house into an oven, but Lizzie's sole con-
cession was to remove the coat and roll the sleeves of the jacket
as she went on bottling cough cures that would do for another
winter.

I worried over Lizzie's past. She resembled Granma in that I
couldn't believe she'd had one. I was sure she'd always been the
same.

Yet there were hints in the house of a Lizzie who'd been different. Here and there, like clues, were objects that linked her
present life to another.

Some of the things Lizzie showed me herself. One day she
opened her hand, and nesting on her palm was a scatter of
gold: a signet-ring engraved with grapes, an Albert watch-chain
dangling a shark's tooth for luck, a stick-pin crowned with a
nugget. She blew the dust from a photograph, and that was the
gentleman the golden horde had belonged to. Once he'd been
Lizzie's husband, and an Englishman with skin even whiter
than Teddy Teakle's—so white it looked green in the shade;
so delicate that on his first day in Australia the sun burnt it to
blisters. He revived, however, in time to join the rush to the Victorian goldfields.

Lizzie made Bendigo sound queer. The ground was hollowed
like a honeycomb; you slept in a tent, every nationality—even
Chinese—huddled in promiscuous confusion. The police had
muskets and fixed bayonets; they put you in a log-house for
misdemeanours ...

Lizzie's voice trailed off. Mr Potter never became a real person. I never knew if he'd dredged up a fortune; what happened
to him, how he'd died. He stayed someone who, unlike Lizzie

and Granma, was possessed only of a past. It was impossible to link that young sepia face with Lizzie's old one.

Sometimes when Lizzie stirred at her latest brew I went into her bedroom. The choice pieces of her collection were there.

A rocking-horse lacking its tail was frozen in full gallop. A glass case held a species of long-legged bird. The brass bed was covered with a quilt gone to moth-holes; the wardrobe was carved with acanthus leaves.

The first time I opened it I got a fright, for something white leapt out. For an instant I feared a ghost, but then I saw it was an old-fashioned dress. Its skirt snapped and crackled. It was either a wedding-dress or a gown of the type that country girls were said to have worn, tied in a figure eight to the saddle, as they rode on horseback to a ball.

Except for the dress, the wardrobe was empty. I wondered if it had been Lizzie's. It seemed impossible that she should ever have fitted inside that tiny bodice, but you never knew. I didn't like to ask her—really, I didn't want to be disillusioned. It was pleasant to nurture the hope that it *had* been hers; that, wearing it, she'd once been as elegant as her Englishman with his lucky shark's tooth and pale green complexion.

4

Rina Todd came to live with Lizzie out of nowhere. One day I knocked at Lizzie's door and it was opened by a stranger—someone tall, with skin the colour of half-done toast. Only Meg liked her toast as pale as that. I ate mine nearly burnt. The toast crumbs, then, were like ants.

The stranger was eating a peach. Her manners were bad. Juice ran down her chin but she didn't care. She chased it lazily with her tongue. She had peach flesh stuck between her teeth.

Lizzie introduced us. Rina Todd popped the peach stone into her mouth and ignored me. Then she spat the stone into her hand and threw it over my head at the sunflowers and the sky. I could see up her sleeve when she did it. There was a black powder-puff up there, shiny with sweat.

No one knew where Rina had come from, or who she was. Some said she was a distant relative from Cudlee Creek—didn't Lizzie have a cousin there? Others hinted the relationship to be closer, and imbued it with a touch of spice—remember the time when Lizzie took in lodgers ... the salesman with the neat little hand-grip—Rina was cast in the role of long lost daughter, returned by an act of God. She was supposed to have been seen walking into town on the Gully Road, limping along without her shoes, crying. Yet the driver of the morning coach swore he'd brought her in himself—she wore a travelling costume of amazon cloth and her hat had a speckled feather. There was even a story the boys whispered at school, about coming across her taking a dip in the creek: stark naked, crowned with lilies. She was said to be Indian, Italian, as Irish as Paddy's pig. The butcher thought he remembered her telling fortunes from tea-leaves in last year's travelling circus; Miss Meek paused in sorting duchesse sets in the draper's to vow she'd seen her on stage at the Theatre Royal. But what was the leading lady of *The Cingalee* doing, incognito, in Fern Gully?

Lizzie kept mum. Rina could have been anyone. She was foreign looking, certainly. There was the Melba toast skin and the big dark eyes. She had twin moles—one on either side of her smile—and masses of hair. Sometimes she looked like a schoolgirl; other times her body nudged her clothes and you knew she was a woman.

Things weren't the same any more.

Now Lizzie's bed had two dents in it instead of one. And my hand didn't touch her old one as we pushed the perambulator to the dump. Now Lizzie's hand was claimed by Rina, and I was left to run behind.

It was Rina who found the ferns that clung to the earth, and the violets that grew by the creek. Soon they were growing in Lizzie's garden with a variety of other plants. For Rina had green fingers and, when she needed it, a silvery tongue. She charmed Mother into giving her an apronful of cuttings. Fuchsias and geraniums flourished inside the cockle-shell borders.

Rina did things inside the house, too. From time to time she'd be taken with an urge to spring-clean. I'd peep over the squeaker hedge to see the rocking-horse standing in the garden and Rina chasing a cloud of dust. Sometimes she liked to cook—but only food that was sweet. For days the kitchen would be scented with chocolate chip kisses and frangipani tart, and Rina and Lizzie would sport matching sugar-crystal moustaches. Then the cooking spell would wear off and Lizzie would return to brewing her stews that tasted of cough syrup.

But, without warning, Rina's capabilities would desert her. Suddenly she'd turn simple-minded. She peed standing up, and forgot to comb her hair. She squatted in the dust or played a game of tig with her shadow.

Perhaps Lizzie loved her most when she went like that. She gathered Rina into her arms and rubbed her with marshmallow ointment; dosed her with Balm of Gilead throat mixture, fed her chamomile tea off a spoon. She tucked Rina under the crazy quilt, and for a week the bedroom curtains stayed drawn.

One Saturday Rina was in the garden, shaking pins from her hair. A bowl of water stood on a table by the grape-vine. As usual, I was ignored. Then Rina started pulling faces, and I thought they were at me till I saw she was having trouble with the pins at the back. She bobbed her head and motioned me over. I pulled them out, one by one, and her hair fell down in a black waterfall. She spoke to me, then; she was nice. She said my hands were gentle, and she bent over the bowl and let me rub with Velvet soap.

But the best part came when she sat on Lizzie's front doorstep. I smoothed her wet hair, coaxing the tangles till they unravelled and some of them were snared by the comb. The hairs floated away like dusky Father Christmas thistles. Rina shut her eyes and the twin moles trembled. She was so happy she started to sing, but the song was sad:

> "I stand in a land of roses,
> But I dream of a land of snow.
> Where you and I were happy,
> In the years of long ago ..."

After that I played hairdresser every Saturday. Rina's hair might have been mine, I knew it so well—all those ringlets and waves, and the frizzy bits low on her forehead, and the prettily tasselled split ends. I tried out latest styles: a soft pompadour, a Psyche knot.

Rina began to trust me. Her mouth came open, she confided. But the more she talked, the more mysterious she became. Did she really know Melbourne so well?—who'd taken her to Menzies' Hotel with its Egyptian Lounge and Winter Garden? Rina liked me so much she showed me the mole on her belly, and let me pluck the fringes of her Chinese shawl. The shawl was lovely. She hinted a gentleman had given it as a present.

When I did her hair in the new Recamier coiffure Rina was more appreciative than ever. She made me sit on her knee and cuddle against her. She held me so tight it was uncomfortable. I had to keep stiff, otherwise my arm would have touched her chest.

Rina was so still I worried she'd gone to sleep; at the same time I fancied she was waiting for me to do something. After a while her eyelashes fluttered, and she put me down. She looked sulky; there were sweat dots above her lip.

I said I'd better go home. Mother was cross if you were late for Saturday dinner.

But Rina slapped my hand, and said, "Oh no, naughty girl, not yet." She said she had a surprise—a nice one. I waited while she ran into the house.

That Saturday we were alone. Lizzie was delivering pile ointment to Miss Meek. It was hot. It felt as if the sun had crept inside my head and was thumping to get out.

Rina tapped my shoulder. She must have tiptoed, she'd come so quietly. She stood there, smiling. "Say I'm beautiful," she said.

She wore Lizzie's dress. Out of the wardrobe it was more yellow than white. The sun slid over the skirt and burnished it to a pale gold. Rina looked like a fiery princess standing in front of the silver house.

I tried not to look at her above waist. The bodice fitted perfectly, but the neck of the dress was rude. Rina pulled it lower. I even saw a nipple. It was hard and brown, like the pimples Lizzie cured with her famous bogbean tea.

"Say it," she said, and now she wasn't smiling. I thought of Mother dishing up dinner—dessert was roly-poly pudding.

She minced towards me, and only stopped when there was a snap and the dress began to split at the seams. I started to cry

26

and she chased me round the water-tank. She caught hold of the tail of my dress and spun me about.

I was frightened. I longed for her to turn safely simple-minded. She did queer things: butterfly-kissed inside my ear, tickled under my skirt. I hated her. I kicked her on the ankle and she let me go. I ran down the path, and didn't feel safe till I was behind the squeaker hedge and could see she wasn't coming.

5

I was scared of the teacher at school. He had a stick that hit you, though his forte—reserved for the boys—was to take hold of an errant scholar's ear and lift him up off his seat.

Mr Kitto was a bachelor, somewhat deformed by a lateral curvature of the spine. He had an irascible disposition and a tendency to grind his teeth.

If you concentrated on his face he was handsome. Teacher's profile would have done justice to any Catholic variety of Jesus; it would have looked good outfitted like wicked Philip's of Spain—complemented by ruff and ear-ring. He had a tan, even when it was winter and other people's skin went pale. His brown eyes were liquid; his beard was only a tuft. When his teeth weren't grinding they stood nicely regular and white.

But when you looked at him whole he was horrid. The crooked spine was emphasized by an awful habit of swaying. His body matched his greasy eyes, his oily skin: it was so supple it seemed double-jointed. More than Jesus and King Philip, Mr Kitto reminded me of a snake. He couldn't keep still. When he talked his body moved in rhythm to his words. Even his fingers made rushing advances on the air.

Mr Kitto taught the big boys and girls. The younger ones were in the charge of a pupil-teacher who, last year, had been a schoolgirl herself. She was scared of Mr Kitto, too. She got the trembles when he watched her lessons. He did that a lot.

For Teacher had a passion for little girls. He surveyed the ranks of the first class with a connoisseur's eye. He liked all sorts—china doll, ingénue, gipsy queen. Even an ugly-duckling appearance couldn't guarantee immunity from his roving fingers. Not that Mr Kitto's fingers did anything nasty—they just liked to splurge out now and then, to indulge in a choice pinch and pat. It was innocent enough. Mothers smirked proudly when it had been *their* little girl who'd been the object of his attentions, and said wasn't it nice how Teacher fancied kiddies ... There was no harm in it, but the little girls shivered when he entered the room and cast his crooked shadow over their desk. The tips of his fingers felt moist. The pinch lingered on too long.

Little boys, however, were a different matter. Mr Kitto's hand didn't extend to them. His stick did instead. Exercising it on little boys' flanks put him in even better humour than pinching. We listened for whacks through the wall. The pupil-teacher trembled and stopped up her ears. Mr Kitto swayed worse than ever when he returned from supervising the infants.

He hit Baby Pettigrew most of all. Baby was really too old to be an infant, but somehow he couldn't learn. He was hopeless at getting dates to heart, or recalling important history facts: "King Henry never smiled again after his son, William, drowned in the Channel", "King John lost his crown in the Wash and died of eating green peaches". So while others his age wrote with a pen in a copy-book, Baby stayed next door where slate-pencils squeaked and wooden beads clicked along counting-frames. If it hadn't been for Mr Kitto venturing there so often I wouldn't have minded keeping him company. It had been pleasant being an infant. I missed the miniature wheat-fields that flourished in saucers of damp wadding on the window-sill, the pickle-jars for flowers; the First Royal Reader, the Sensible Spelling Book; the picture by the door of Moses in the Den of Lions.

Now, instead of Moses, Queen Victoria stared down at us. She didn't look happy in her picture. Her mouth was tucked in, disapproving; there were fly-specks on her pale blue sash. Why did it have to be her up there—why not dainty Alexandra with her swan's neck encased in pearls?

But the old Queen's expression suited the schoolroom. Anything extraneous to learning had been swept away; there were no flowers, no saucers of wheat. Sometimes, in dreams, the schoolroom turned into a torture chamber. Maybe that was because of Mr Kitto's invention. He complained we tended to hunch over our desks, noses almost touching our books. He provided us each with a thin piece of fencing wire, fifteen inches long, to one end of which was fixed a cork. By placing the cork against your forehead, and the other end of the wire on the desk, the proper distance between eye and page was ascertained. In my dreams the cork usually fell of, and wire neatly dislodged an eye.

The man on the oilcloth chart didn't help, either, to make the schoolroom a comfortable place. He was bigger than life-size, and at first glance appeared normal—though lacking his clothes, and decidedly androgynous below waist. Then Mr Kitto's hand came out and seized a little flap, and then another: the man on the chart was peeled of his skin, to become a layer of muscle ... then a series of arteries and veins, finally a skeleton.

Although I liked learning, I thought a lot about leaving school. Then I would be quite safe. Mr Kitto, and everything else unpleasant, would be blocked out by the familiarities of home. I conveniently ignored the squeaker hedge down the lane, and the presence of Rina and Lizzie behind it. After all, now I only saw them small, from a distance. I hardly felt a twinge of guilt when I remembered the last time I'd seen Lizzie in her garden—and then, as she raised her head, lowered mine, and pretended I hadn't. Somehow, because of the day when Rina put on the wedding-dress, Lizzie had turned into someone to be avoided.

The only thing that worried me about leaving school was what would happen to Baby Pettigrew. With me gone, who would protect him? For I could never imagine Baby's life changing as mine would. The years might pass but he would remain the same: perpetually childlike, with an over-large head and sleepy eyes.

I first made Baby's acquaintance in the schoolyard. Near

the infants' room was a water-butt for supplying drinks. From time to time a drinking mug was provided, attached to the cask with a chain. But that would soon disappear, and then drinking vessels were extemporised. While the cask was nearly full your hands would do, but as the level fell papers folded into ships and military hats were used.

One recess-time there was more commotion than usual round the water-butt. I ran over and saw a pair of struggling legs. They were Baby's. The school bully had him up on his shoulders and he was halfway plunged towards a ducking. Everyone was laughing, but I felt virtuous as I hit Bully Edwards with my lunch tin.

Baby became my friend. The nicest thing about him was that you could make him into anything you wished. He was docile, accommodating. He would shrink small, and I'd rock him in my arms and pretend he was my child. He allowed me to lower his trousers and inspect the witchetty-grub growth secreted there.

Baby's real name was Alfred. Long ago his parents had been converted at a religious revival. Baby's big sisters were called Love and Mercy, but by the time he was born religion had lost its appeal. Some people said Alfred's condition was a punishment. Mr Pettigrew drank and was an idler, though he didn't have a bad leg to plead his cause like Father. And Mrs Pettigrew couldn't command respect like Mother because of coming into *her* mother's money. Now and then she scrubbed floors, but mostly she was as indolent as her husband. If it hadn't been for Love and Mercy, the family would have been in the poorhouse.

Love and Mercy had reputations. As well, they had silk stockings and amber hat-pins.

Love was exotic, with oriental eyes. She favoured dramatic effects. Snowy veils embroidered with fruit and flowers hung from her picture-hats. Whenever she passed a gentleman, she had a trick of flinging up the veil to disclose her face.

Mercy was blonde, and tucked bunches of violets in the neck

of her dresses. Like Love, she assisted Nature liberally with *poudre de riz* and bloom of Ninon. She had a turkey-down boa, and when she kissed you her tongue tasted of icing-sugar.

I enjoyed kissing Baby's sisters. They said I was good to practise on. When they kissed me—when Mercy plucked under her arms with the tweezers, and Love's kimono came open and I saw she had nothing on underneath—it wasn't rude. Love and Mercy were nothing to do with Rina Todd. I didn't care what Meg said about them; or that I could never let Mother and Father know I visited Pettigrews'.

Their part of the house was spotless. You'd never have believed that Love and Mercy's snuggery could have existed so close to squalor. One minute you were surrounded by dust and grease spots, the next you opened a door and there were satin bedspreads and gipsy tables, and the accumulated gleams of crystal—fruit dishes, salad bowls, sparklets—and silver—butter dishes, jam spoons, biscuit barrels.

The crystal- and silver-ware were presents from admirers; Love and Mercy said they were saving for their glory boxes. Sometimes I saw some of the gentlemen arrive. I never knew their names, for they scuttled in very discreet, breathing into their collars. I suspected what Love and Mercy let them do, but I didn't care. When they left, Baby's sisters were nicer than ever. They shared out chocolates and sips of ginger wine. There was usually something new in the way of knick-knacks to approve.

6

But Mr Kitto wasn't all ogre. On Friday afternoons he improved. He lay down his stick, and rolled up the oilcloth man, and didn't quibble as our noses crept nearer to our books. He stopped grinding his teeth; the tempo of his swaying diminished. He sank into his chair and entertained us with a repertoire of curious facts.

Fancy—that among the exhibits at the Southend Chrysanthemum Society's show of flowers and fruit was once a bunch of grapes grown from a pip thrown in the garden after the stoning of raisins for a Christmas pudding. And would you believe that only one man in a thousand in the Russian Army possessed a handkerchief? And how handy to know that if your bicycle light suddenly failed, you might remedy the mishap by placing a glow-worm or two within the glass.

It was Mr Kitto who organized the school band, and drilled the kettledrums in long rolls and flamboyant paradiddles; and transformed the school earth-closets with a regular supply of ashes and a swilling with strong disinfectant; and initiated the School Picnic Trip to Glenelg.

Now the picnic had become an annual event. Old as well as present scholars looked forward eagerly to the day, and all the grown-ups who could manage joined in, too.

The picnic of 1906 was the last one I went to. As usual, it was an adventure getting up so early that the sky was still pale, and there was only a quiver of heat in the air. We assembled outside the Institute Hall at seven o'clock, precisely. Everyone was dressed up; it might have been Sunday. I wore my best white frock. It was funny looking down and watching my legs marching along in black stockings under a skirt starched as stiff as cardboard.

Mother had removed the hairs above her lip with Pelox; Father sported a rosebud buttonhole; Meg did us proud with her belt pulled in tight to make a weeny waist.

Mr Kitto darted about, his hands rhapsodic, as they shepherded a flock of little girls into the first of the drags. Miss Meek had forgone duchesse sets and embroidery thread to rub elbows with Love and Mercy. Baby appeared more foolish than usual, rigged out in a sailor suit and a straw hat whose ribbon proclaimed H.M.S. INDOMITABLE. Beside me, Meg lowered her eyes as she sighted Teddy Teakle, fittingly attired in regatta shirt and striped holland suit.

Soon the road was slipping away before us. Now the sky was bright blue, and the sun felt hot. The horses' heads were swathed with fern to keep off the flies.

There was so much to look at, that the journey to Adelaide seemed short. As we turned into Rundle Street, where the big shops were hailed with a cheer, I looked over my shoulder and saw faraway hills at its end. They were my hills—The Hills— but now they'd turned small and toy-like. They might have been modelled from papier-mâché.

Victoria Square was full of statues. The old Queen perched aloft, mimicking her schoolroom demeanour in bronze; explorers were frozen in hero poses.

There were inviting patches of shade under the trees but we ignored them, for there was also a train standing ready. The train meant the beach. We clambered from the drags without a backward glance, and helter-skelter jumped on board.

Even that trip had its romance. For a while we steamed past thick clumps of trees, the last remnant of the notorious Black Forest, once the hiding place of cattle stealers and like desperadoes.

At last we reached Glenelg, where another round of cheering greeted the briny.

Mr Kitto led us over the sand. We wove our way between other picnic parties and an assortment of horse-drawn vehicles.
Soon we'd claimed a portion of beach for the Gully. Rugs were
spread out, and canvas awnings erected. To start with, everyone
was stiff, self-conscious. People remembered who they were
supposed to be, and kept playing out their everyday roles. Miss
Meek seemed to prefer the landscape of her lap to the bigger
world about her; the Pettigrew sisters kept smiling; Meg played
lady beneath her sunshade. But, gradually, people were affected by the queerness of it all—the great expanse of sky and sea,
so unfamiliarly open after the Hills, where you were hemmed
in by trees and small-town eyes; the beach with its passing parade of strangers. Sand sifted into their clothes and the sun got
at their skin. People began to change: shed identity, turn anonymous. Miss Meek exposed her arms above elbow.

Baby and I set off to explore. There was so much to choose
from, we didn't know which way to go.

If you put your stockings on, and brushed away the sand it
was permissible to walk along the Esplanade, where ladies resembled fashion-plates and there were Oyster Saloons and Refreshment Rooms and all the other accessories of a select marine
retreat. Or you could stay dishevelled, and paddle in the shallows
and examine the curious encrustations of barnacles on the piles
of the jetty, while above your head you heard the tap of people's
feet as they stepped out over the sea. You could join them, and
wave to steamers setting off for Kangaroo Island, and listen to the
Adelaide Glee Club and the Holdfast Model Band take turns in
giving a concert. To either side of the jetty was the most exten-
sive Natatorium in the world. You paid sixpence, and swam in a
cage—ladies to the left, gentlemen to the right; afterwards, you
took a hot seawater shower and, to obtain maximum health ben-
efit, put your clothes on over the salt. There were shooting galler-
ies and merry-go-rounds and—inside a tent by the sea wall—a
public entertainer, hypnotized by his wife on Christmas Eve, was
in a trance till New Year's Night.

Mother's egg sandwiches tasted lovely after so much sea air. I shared mine with Baby, whose were only tomato sauce. There was Woodroofe's lemonade to drink; then sandcastles to build and shells to collect in a bucket. As a bonus there were people to watch.

You could lie on the rug next to Mother, and pretend to be sleeping, while you peeped out under your lashes. You saw some good things. Who would have thought Miss Meek's legs were so fat at the top that they bulged over her garters, all wobbly? What a poppy-show! It wasn't your fault that you saw—she shouldn't have been bending over. And what about Mr Kitto?—whispering by the sea wall into Mercy Pettigrew's ear. He appeared as much hypnotized as the public entertainer inside his tent. Mercy whispered back, and once, you could have sworn, her hand came out to give his lateral curvature a fondle. But the most agreeable peep of all was provided by Meg and Teddy. The picnic appeared to have done the trick: Teddy had spoken, and now they were friends. When no one saw but you, they linked little fingers. You weren't surprised—it was fitting they should declare their love here (surely that was what the finger-linking signified?). Glenelg was where you'd allowed they should live after the wedding. You concentrated on the house with its Marseilles tiles and fretwork kanga. There was time to add a candle-snuffer turret before you fell asleep.

Coolness crept into the air and the sun floated low, like a fiery balloon. Then it turned wobbly, dented: more like a mandarin orange. Then it sank further down, and was a slice of watermelon floating on the waves. Then the waves swallowed it up, and the sky blushed fuchsia-pink.

People stirred themselves, and woke from dreaming. For a while their eyes were dazed, and their faces stayed innocent. Then a child whimpered, a dog raced over the sand. "The tide's coming in," someone murmured. Anonymity fled. The soft bundle I lay against turned into Mother. She was dressed up:

she wore her best brooch that was a gold map of Australia and a boomerang and a row of letters that said DINNA FORGET. But if you looked hard you saw that Cape York Peninsula was dented, and along her top lip was a stubby line of hairs—the Pelox hadn't done much of a job. Mother was flawed, and so was everyone else. The picnic trip was almost over. People masked their faces with workaday expressions. Miss Meek twitched at the gores of her skirt and rolled down her sleeves; Mr Kitto positioned himself a long way from Mercy Pettigrew.

We gathered up our things. The day had changed into evening, and I felt melancholy.

It would have been all right if I'd been home, flinging knives and forks at the tablecloth, anticipating Delicious Pudding or Sago Cream. The glow of the kerosene lamp would have comforted me, and a read of one of Meg's *Girl's Own Annuals*, and giving the back verandah pot plants a watering. The water would have sunk into the earth with a dotted sound, almost a buzz; the rubbery, lacy leaves would have looked cool; I would have felt like me—Thea Hodge: twelve years old and someone, up to my last year at school. Home was cosy and safe; in it you knew who you were. Here, at the beach, day-time gone and night not yet come to blot everything out, you existed only as an afterthought.

The sea sucked at the shore, and we trudged away. All that was left of the picnic were hollows in the sand, orange peel, lolly papers.

7

I loved reading the *Observer*. It came every Saturday. Its pages told stories that rivalled those of Mother and the brothers Grimm.

There was something on every page. Who was Oskar Karlowitch Grosse, earnestly requested in the column for Missing Friends, to communicate with the Imperial Consul for Russia, in Sydney? Dear Oskar—what a nice name—I saw him in dashing navy breeches with a scarlet stripe at the side. Even the advertisements put pictures in my head: "Ostrich plumes from the famous farms of South Africa ... There is nothing more becoming to the average woman than the soft setting given her face by really good feathers". Very well, then—I chose black and white mixed. They bobbed as I shed tears, but remained forget-me-not eyed, over my poor pallid loved one, off to join the other consumptives at Kalyra Sanatorium, Belair (the insert said to write for terms). Even Little Leo Nankivell, who featured week after week, guaranteed a pleasant shudder: "... Convulsions when a baby—took fits in his sleep—suffered for years—wasted to skin and bone—strong healthy lad today: DR. WILLIAMS' PINK PILLS".

I read the newspaper, and wondered if anything was wrong with my life; if anything was wrong with Mother's and Father's and Meg's. Why was Mother so content, darning on a wooden mushroom, biting at thread with her teeth, flinging one stocking down, reaching for the next? Why had the Hills been all she'd ever wanted? Why had she been so unhappy at Prospect, even though there were Madonna lilies in the garden, and butcher and baker called daily?

Prospect had been an assortment of people ... a postman in

a scarlet coat who brought your letters to the door, and a Chinese pedlar whose lacquered cabinets were suspended from a pole across his shoulders. You called "Ching Chong Chinaman" and—if you were brave—"Yeller Belly" when he was safely out the gate, but his things were nice: lace and jars of ginger, pink toothpaste, and feather dusters. There'd been an organ-grinder with a monkey in a military jacket who presented arms with a little wooden musket. There were foreigners, bigger than Chinky-Chinaman, who were dangerous. The Turkey Lolly Man sold jujubes, and Meg said never to take one, for they were drugged, and you'd wake up in the harem where they did the belly-dance. An Italian lady, all in black, carried a basket of trimmings for hats—bunches of wax cherries, veils specked with miniature pom-poms. But the cherries and veiling were part of her disguise. She was really the Gipsy Queen—Meg knew that, too—come to steal you away.

Prospect had meant the lamplighter on his bicycle at dusk; bullocks being driven down the Lower North Road to the slaughter yard every Monday (Tuesday was sheep on their way to market); the Lavatory Man who came at night to collect the contents of the bucket-privy. Prospect was the smell of beer from the hotel—an interesting smell that clung to your nose, but Mother pulled you past; you knew she hated living next door. But, most of all, Prospect was trams. And trams meant Father.

I looked forward to holding Mother's hand and waiting for one to come ... wondering which it would be—single-decker or double?—bearing which advertisements—Mellin's Food for Infants, Fry's Cocoa? So many things were part of the ritual: both of us dressed in our best, for we were on our way to the city; Mother peering in her purse to make sure she had the block of tram-tickets that resembled postage stamps. We always sat in the saloon with its scent of cigarettes and wax polish, stale perfume and sweat. Though the seats were hard the cherrywood panelling was handsome. I always hoped the driver might be

Father—it never was. But I didn't stay disappointed for long; there was so much else to look forward to. In Brougham Gardens, going downhill, the hand-brake was screwed on to prevent the tram running on to the horses' heels; near the Cathedral one of the auxiliary hill horses waited to help in the pull up King William Road. It was my job to present our tickets to the conductor. He was usually a gawky youth whose trousers didn't meet his boot tops, but he registered fares importantly; he wore all the letters of the company's name round the band of his hat.

I assured Mother that a tram was better than a victoria, even a Rosa buggy. Mother only shrugged. When Father had his accident she'd cried, but I knew part of her wasn't sorry. For no more trams meant no more life at Prospect.

The accident had been written up in the newspaper. Mother had cut the paragraph out and put it inside her Bible with the bits of pressed silver-paper and bridesmaid's fern. That was the only time Father's life had rivalled Little Leo Nankivell's and Oskar Karlowitch Grosse's in making news.

Prospect had been a long way off when Mother and Father met. He'd come to the Gully for the apple picking, and Mother's story insisted on love at first sight. I didn't doubt her, though she improved on Nature by muddling the seasons, and offset her upward-gazing face by adding a mess of descending petals to a harvest of Jonathans and Cleos. Father had apparently looked down from his ladder and been instantly smitten. Mother hadn't demanded a long courting, a prolonged spell of playing handies. She'd defied Granma's tirade about Bowden and questionable origins. Really, it sounded as if she'd run away from home; eloped with Father into the Mallee. Which sounded like another country, but Meg said was only trees.

Mother still had her wedding bouquet—a few sprigs of wax-cloth orange blossom, she kept in a cardboard box under the bed. Two days after the wedding they came down to the city, and dressed up in their finery again. In the photo that hung on the bedroom wall Mother's bouquet was a big one of exotic studio blooms.

The people in the photograph were strangers. I disregarded the out-of-date clothes, and the shadowy backdrop that suggested somewhere Alpine, and concentrated on their features. Father didn't even have a beard to hide behind. His face was a boy's; his hair cocked up on top, as if he'd combed it through with sugar and water, then dented in a wave. Beside him on the studio rustic bridge, Mother made a try at appearing demure. She didn't succeed, though, because of her lip. The night before, it had come out in a boil. No amount of chewing on nutmeg would help.

It was hard to picture Father up north clearing scrubland for wheat with a stump-jump plough; harder to see Mother glorying in the queer blow-about bushes of skeleton weed and the clouds of tiny flies.

Yet Mother had fought the Mallee with imagination. She shooed the flies with a turkey-wing fan and sewed a series of fetching piqué hats to hide her complexion from the sun. When Meg was born she made Father tie a white ribbon to the gate— it was an old English custom, she said, and signified baby was a girl. One Christmas there was a drought; meat was scarce, and Mother had no fat to make the plum pudding. But she wouldn't be beaten. A tallow candle cut up fine did just as well; and, anyway, who cared about the pudding's taste? The main thing was the lucky charms that went in, too.

Out in the Mallee, Mother began telling her stories. If you looked on the bright side, words could do wonders. "Humble cot" was so much nicer than "hut"... after all, the climbing rose might survive the summer, the slips of fuchsia might take. The marcella quilt suspended on saplings was a verandah to sit under while you waited for the cool change to come. And didn't everyone say dear hubby resembled the Prince of Wales?—especially now he'd grown the beard. And even though Mama forgot to write, it didn't mean she didn't care. Your hands weren't ruined from housework. Though your eyes were perpetually squinting against the glare you didn't have hardly a wrinkle.

The stories became a habit. They accompanied us on the move to Prospect; ventured into the Hills. Mother told them as she stuck the layers of marble cake together with jam, as she slipped another stocking over the wooden mushroom. She fantasized so persistently that I couldn't concentrate on the *Observer*. My ostrich plumes stopped bobbing; my loved one's hanky was cheated of its final benediction of blood.

Mother didn't just make her stories up; she went one better than the brothers Grimm. She spun fantasies out of hard facts. She had no need of goose girls and robber-bridegrooms; she did wonders with a strictly limited cast, linked by ties of family or the boundaries of the Gully.

Lately the stories featured Meg. Nothing much happened to her. She didn't bite on a poisoned apple, or have a try at spinning gold from straw. Mother's prattling was all a variation on a theme. How and when, where and why Meg ended up as Mrs Teakle.

Mother was clever and a good Methodist, too. She mingled fact and fantasy judiciously; yet she took care you should know where conjecture began. When it was a matter of detail—what dress Meg wore, how she'd done her hair—she always got it right. If Mother conjured her up playing the piano, you knew that, if it was a sacred solo, the music book had "Bowden" scored out on the cover, that its spine was reinforced with a velvet strip. If a plot demanded she be returning from her day doing anatomy at the School of Design, Mother peeped under her gloves and put in the conté smudges on her fingers.

Apart from the acknowledged flights of fancy that got Meg to the altar, Mother never told a lie. She didn't need to. Not when leaving things out was just as good.

That was what worried me. Not the happy-ever-after endings, one of which was bound to come true. I'd settled Meg

with Teddy under Marseilles tiles countless times myself. But
in my stories Meg had some flaws. I couldn't forget the way she
sneered at Baby, how she'd told on me for doing wee in the
bath. And what about the face powder she didn't always use
invisibly; the handkerchiefs she put inside her bodice to assist
it to a swan's-breast swell?

The trouble with Mother's stories was that they made the
real world seem wrong. Meg wasn't merely a dressmaker's dum-
my or an angel in disguise. I hated going in the lav after her, she
sometimes left such a smell. Once a month she had to lie on her
bed, and I saw the stain on her bloomers.

And what about the meetings with Teddy?

Poor Mother seemed to think that part of the story true—
where Meg sat on one side of the table for afternoon-tea, and
Mr Teakle the other. He smiled as he passed the plate of rockies,
and told her she resembled his dear dead wife. He showed her
over the jam factory, and gave her a tin of apricot to take home
to Mother. He said, Would you like a flower from the conserva-
tory? He said, Child, I declare, you will make Teddy the perfect
helpmate.

Mr Teakle didn't even know Meg existed. Each week at
church he cut her dead. On Sundays, glued to his father's elbow,
Teddy only spared her a nod. Their courtship stayed unofficial.
He never took her anywhere, he never came to the house. They
met at the top of the lane. Meg took care she wore an old dress
then. Something good might get torn pushing through all those
briers to reach the wattle and daub hut.

Meg was cross when I asked her if they weren't scared going
in. No one had lived there for years—not since the gentleman,
who lost his hand in the winnower, died. Weren't they scared he
might visit the place as a spirit? What if he tapped them with
his hook?—though the dinner fork would be worse.

Meg said, "We never did. Teddy and I never went there."
Then she changed her mind. She said it was a secret. That Teddy was painting her portrait. It was a surprise and would be in

the Autumn Exhibition at the Royal Society of Arts. She gave me her lucky clover brooch. She said, "Promise you won't tell. Never ever."

Something was wrong with life. Nothing was happening as it should. I knew, without Mother's stories assuring me, that Meg was meant for that perfect white wedding. Yet when would it come? Why didn't Teddy ask her? And if the wedding wasn't with Teddy, who else would do? There wasn't another in the Gully good enough, and it seemed mostly ladies did artistic anatomy and repoussé at the School of Design.

Sometimes I thought only Father could help Meg. Mother lived in a dreamland, I was too young to offer advice. Father loved her best of all. He would have killed anyone who hurt her.

But Father had already been hurt himself. It wasn't just the accident and having to leave the trams. Not even that could have humbled him so much. The way he looked at Meg—as if he couldn't believe his luck they were related—made me feel like crying. It was precisely because Father knew how dreams turned leaden, how life went sour if you didn't approach it right, that he'd never be able to make Meg see things as they really were. He wasn't brave enough to be cruel.

Once at school Bully Edwards sniggered, and the boys looked at me like they did at Baby, when Mr Kitto inspected his head and said it would have to be shaved. I heard Bully say the words behind his hand—he meant me to. At Prospect you called out "Yeller Belly" when it was a Chinese. What did "Wine-dot" have to do with Father?

Mercy Pettigrew said a wine-dot was someone who drank. A blackfellow, a dirty old man. In Adelaide they called that part of the Torrens where the wineohs went, Pinky Flat.

But Father didn't drink. Well, hardly. Beer didn't count; but the other—the smell was nasty. He hid the bottle by the fowl-house. He thought I didn't see. But his hand went into the daisy bush and he pulled it out as if it was precious. And his hands were rubbing the bottle as if he was playing nurse. He didn't

come in for his tea. Mother didn't ask where he was. She just
sighed and told Meg that Marshall's had some nice taffeta-voil-
le in their sale. His plate stayed on top of the stove. The meat
went shrivelled; the peas were little pellets. I didn't hear him
come in, but in the morning there was the smell the same as always—queer: perfume and cough mixture and sick, combined.
And Mother was washing his shirt at the sink. And he didn't get
up till late. When he did his cheeks were sunken, because he
hadn't put in his teeth.

Was that being a wine-dot? Only now and then? And, anyway, it wasn't wine Father drank out of the bottle. The label said
Buchanan's whisky.

But a whineoh—someone who took too much pinky, got
shickered—wasn't like Father. When Mr Pettigrew got under
the influence he came home and smashed things up. Father
never did that. He was even sick discreetly. There was only
the smell afterwards, and his shirt flapping on the line, all evidence of dribbles washed away. Father was gentle. When it was
Christmas or a birthday Mother had to kill the fowl. When the
spoggy flew in at the window and thumped against the pane,
Father couldn't touch it. Nor the moth that stayed still on the
dining-room wall. Mother crushed it as easy as winking with
her shoe.

Father never touched a drop in Mother's stories (she had
to think of his dignity, now he bore resemblance to a king, not
merely the Prince of Wales). He was always aged about twenty,
with a shamrock tie-pin, without a beard; always looking down
on her from a ladder, with his lovely eyes. As for conjecture ...
well, she told Miss Meek that he was thinking of emulating the
late Duke of Cambridge, and writing his memoirs—it was just
a matter of putting pen to paper. For Father, she even risked
a lie. She said it was in bad taste to tell, but he'd got his crippled leg by being a hero ..."Well, no, Miss Meek, I cannot exactly say. But it was saving the life of a kiddy. Dear little chap
... highborn." She said a letter had come from Lord Tennyson,

who was Governor at the time. It was delightful at his summer residence—all those camellias, such statuary.

Sometimes Father wrapped apples: Grannies, Delicious, Rome Beauty ... those ones with the foreign name: Gravenstein, that ripened early, and were yellowy-green with red stripes. Sometimes he sold the plums from the trees at the back to Teakle's. Once he'd put in a spell as temporary inspector for codlin-moth. It was lucky he'd had Granma's house and money to count on. Especially since his favourite occupation had become leafing through the almanac. He said it was full of the world's wonders, as good as a trip overseas. He sat at the kitchen table and pondered moons and tides.

In the *Observer* other people's lives were different. Miss Wilhelmina Kohl, sixteen, jumped into the Torrens, scattering a confused medley of Scripture texts behind her (postmortem examination revealed signs of an indisposition of two months' standing). Mrs Stow, of Childers Street, North Adelaide, went to the seaside for a change. Miss Bessie Davidson and Miss Rose MacPherson, whose pictures were accepted by the Paris Salon, returned to the land of their birth laden with the artistic thoughts of several years. Walter Munro, twenty-three, was found in the chaff-house of the Globe Hotel, Wallaroo, with a bullet through his right temple.

People took strychnine and got bitten by poisonous spiders; served sumptuous teas on Walkerville verandahs, were presented with illuminated addresses in folding morocco covers. But at the Gully nothing happened. Teddy sent Meg a picture of Love's Thermometer on a postcard, and indicated his temperature had reached the zenith of affection's height, but he didn't pop the question. Sometimes Father stopped reading the almanac, and cleared his throat as if he had something to say ... then his eyes met Meg's and flinched: he went back to ruminating equinox and solstice. Mother was on about weddings again, but like Teddy she didn't name a date. Time was passing. The summer holidays were nearly over. "Oh, please God," I prayed, "be fair. Let something happen."

8

Christmas was over, and the picnic, too. The twenty-eighth had been Commemoration Day, and because of 1906 it was special, for the state was seventy years of age and King Edward sent a message of congratulation. On New Year's Eve the public entertainer woke from his trance at Glenelg, and the Gully celebrated in the schoolroom with a children's concert, comprising choruses and fairy songs.

It was school holidays, everything seemed half-asleep. Only nature was busy. There were flowers on the berry bushes; the roses came out.

Sometimes the sun was an enemy. You went outside, and it was like putting your head in an oven—even in the Hills. You walked in the shade, but you were hot.

The sun made you feel small and unimportant. The green patches of England were islands, surrounded by so much that was Australian. All the grass was bleached. Only the clumps of fennel kept their colour, but even they were turning rusty at the bottom.

You fought the sun by standing the milk jug in a basin of water and pulling down the blinds and putting cucumber peel on your forehead, but it could make you afraid. Not merely explorers died of sunstroke.

There was danger in other things, too.

Bushfires started suddenly and unexpectedly, and spread with wonderful rapidity. During the Seven-Year Drought there were perpetual dust-storms and siroccos.

And you mustn't eat the lilies by the creek, for there was a man who did, and he wandered in a dream saying the sun was the moon. Likewise, though oleanders were pretty—crimson and white and palest pink—you mustn't suck a petal or a leaf. Once there was a picnic, and everyone died because someone stirred the billy tea with a twig.

The holidays went on. The creek dried up; the rose by the verandah withered.

I read a lot and squeezed the blackheads on my nose. I learned to make almond crunchies; I began a crewel-work curtain border. But it was more fun finding out what would happen to the King of the Golden Mountain. And playing chasey and hidey with Baby—even though mother frowned, and said I was too old. Next birthday I'd be thirteen: not a child, not anything; now and then I cried. One day Mother caught me and said I needed a change. She could do with one herself. Very well, then, we'd splurge on a visit to the city. The shops. Bricknell's Café. A peep into the Arcade.

The city bore the name of an English queen. It had a Cathedral and a Lunatic Asylum; a Deaf and Dumb mission, and a statue of Robbie Burns. St Peter's College was as good as Eton. There was a Carnation Show in the Town Hall every year.

It was strange that the sun should still assault you in Adelaide; shine so hard that the steps of buildings—even the G.P.O. with its Victoria Tower, even Mrs Powis Stuart's Elocution and Shakespearian Studio on North Terrace—went like silver and seemed to float. And you felt as small as you did in the Hills. All the people in their fashions just like Paris couldn't help. They looked ugly, as if their clothes were cages.

It was hotter than when we'd gone on the picnic; the sky above King William Street was terribly blue. The sale flag was out over John Martin's; Mr Lex McLean—the Scottish Hercules, the Prince of Strongmen—was on the bill at the Hippodrome; you could purchase a pair of elevators at the Federal Boot Company, to raise your height quite an inch. There were all these products of civilization, and the buildings cast long shadows, but still the sun got through—made sweat patches come under ladies' arms, caused gentlemen to remove their jackets.

I liked having holidays, but I wished summer would turn into autumn. Or that spring had stayed. The city was safe in spring—eating Madeira cake after shopping; admiring the plants in the florist's, all of them tagged with proper English-garden names. You felt proud of being where Baroness Burdett-Coutts' money had endowed a See, and the Volunteer Band played on Queen Alexandra's birthday. Anything seemed possible under spring's sky of delicate egg-shell blue. Meg would get married, Father give up drink, Mother stay the same ... holding my hand, saying "What about a glass of lemonade?"

But after the lemonade Mother turned traitor, and made me walk all the way to the cemetery. She said it was just a fancy, a sudden urge. She said Granma and Granpa Hodge and dear old Aunty Vi were there. She didn't seem to notice the sky getting bluer and bigger; that other people had stopped walking beside us, that West Terrace went on for ever. That the cemetery was awful. Unsafe.

At first it pretended not to be. There was this cottage where the caretaker lived, with a pointy roof like the witch's house in Hansel and Gretel. There was a shiny hedge—a squeaker hedge, like Lizzie's. There were borders of salvia and pansy, and a man going snip with secateurs. He wished Mother Good afternoon, and I thought it would be all right. Though the broken column was erected by officers and men on the Overland Telegraph Line in memory of comrades treacherously murdered by the blacks, there was also the grave for Governor Grey's little boy, and lots of the names were out of the Social Page: Jesus was near. But Mother couldn't remember the row. We kept on walking. Even into the Roman Catholic section, where names were Murphy and Donahue, and they had the cheek to impose on your charity, and demand a prayer for the repose of souls.

We had left the city behind; strayed into another land. Though the sun shone hard it wasn't Australia. Everything was

muddled together: the Irish names, and—as well as china flowers and tin leaves with serrated edges: pussy-tails, convolvulus,
umbrella grass. There was a chapel, carved round with sticky-
beak faces. Mother said they were gargoyles, but the fancy
name didn't make me feel better. Palm-trees stood in pools of
tufted shade; a rabbit skipped behind a clump of aloes.

There weren't any more graves, but Mother walked on. Her
good kid shoes were covered in dust; they trod on bull-ants
and rabbit droppings but she didn't notice. Then the crickets
stopped shrilling, the grass petered out. The earth stretched on,
but it was covered with blackened stubble. The grass had been
burnt away; in some parts the earth still smouldered. I hated
being there. It was wrong: one part with posies in vases that
were good enough for the dining-room table, another resembling a view of Hell.

And I thought of the battle-field where Uncle Will had died;
and he wasn't a hero, only a frightened boy. I felt as bad as I did
when Mr Kitto licked his lips and told of Tasmania and the con-
victs getting the whip. Or—though not as bad—when the poets
forsook King Arthur and daffodils, and celebrated four-legged
mates and eating damper. There was wattle in the poems, but
the land was always the colour of khaki. That wasn't my country,
nor this. There was nothing to have a try at shielding me from
the sun: no buildings, no trees like in the Hills. And Mother,
who said a tan was unbecoming, had brought me here.

I said I wanted a drink, I said the sun was hurting my head.
Mother looked surprised to see I was there, even though she
held my hand. But my voice seemed to wake her up. She tutted
over the state of her shoes, and said Didn't it look terrible—that
burnt bit. She said Blow Gran and Granpa and Vi; we'd wasted
enough time already. We turned, and there was grass again, and
the year before last poor Eddie had died, and Flo had erected
a stone carved with words: "Four years his sweetheart, Soon to
have been his bride: But Death's angel claimed him, And took
him from my side."

That was lovely. "The Sick Stockrider" and "How We Beat the Favourite" couldn't compare.

9

A little rain fell, then the sun shone on, and the trees were clotted with fruit. The cherry crop was a good one; the plums were coming along nicely and the apricots looked equally well. The codlin-moth put in an appearance among the apples, but Father routed the pest with arsenical spray.

Mother put on her big check apron and began making jam. At Teakle's they did the same.

From seven in the morning till six at night teams were continually going backward and forward, carting sugar and coal from Port Adelaide, and empty jam tins from the city, as well as fruit and wood from nearer afield. With the aid of twelve steam-coppers 94,400 pounds of raspberries and 5,200 cases of apricots were converted into jam. Every apricot had to be split by the hand, the stone removed, and the kernel cracked: a lot of the girls and boys from school spent their holidays doing it. The last week in January plums began to ripen: the factory aimed at securing 20,000 cases. The road was choked with vehicles, as the growers delivered their fruit.

Things began to happen in other places than the Gully Road.

There was a grass fire at Golden Grove, and a diamond-head snake bit the butcher's finger (he recovered), and Lizzie Potter died.

It was wash day, and nicely windy. The whites flew high. The sheets cracked like trolley-drivers' whips; the tablecloths reared upon the hedge. The coloureds and woollens were pegged on the lines that threaded among the fruit-trees, and even they gave a ripple.

The tea-towels were made of linen that dried stiff. It was my job to beat them soft with a little mallet. I was doing that, and singing "While Choirs of Angels" to keep up the rhythm, when I felt someone standing beside me.

Rina Todd didn't speak. I didn't feel too afraid. She couldn't harm me while I had the mallet; while I was in my own back garden, with the tea-towels spread on the fig-tree stump, and the bantam roosters rambling in the grass. Mother and Meg were under the apple-trees, attending to the family flannels. I could see Mother with her arms inside the body of Father's shirt, stretching with care.

Rina had the same queer smile on her face as last time, though now her nipple was covered.

Mother and Meg started up the path. As they came closer, and were slapped in the face by the sheets, Rina stopped smiling and turned distraught. If I hadn't distrusted her, and seen the smile, I might have cried in sympathy myself. She did it so well. And her face stayed beautiful.

Mother ran forward. It was to her that Rina sobbed the story—how Lizzie and she had been gathering herbs by the creek, and coming back with the perambulator Lizzie had fallen. She wouldn't get up.

Father went to the creek, and returned to say she was dead; then he was off again to fetch Doctor from town. It didn't seem that he'd spoken of anyone I knew. All I felt was anger that Rina should be with us, sitting in the front room with her ankles neatly crossed.

You'd never have thought her a loony. Her little finger cocked genteelly at the handle of her tea-cup; one of the best china plates balanced on her knee. She braced herself against art serge cushions, and played her part with aplomb. One minute her voice was decidedly wheedling as it complimented Mother on the quality of her Roman cutwork, her copper fern bowl, her carved wooden bellows; the next it went tragic as she dutifully recalled her loss, and mourned a Lizzie I'd never known.

The false words wiped out the strong red hands and the wise

creased face, and the deep hollow in the bed where two bodies had curled together. Rina, demure in a girlish pinafore, artfully catching tear-drops on her tongue, reduced Lizzie to the status of dear old Gran. Grudgingly, I admired her versatility, as she changed rôles with quicksilver ease. Now—the last tear winked away, the hanky back up her sleeve—she bravely made the best of things, and declared anguish to have turned her famished ... She knew herself to be a pig, but how she doted on Mother's meringues.

Lizzie had died. There'd be a funeral, and her cousin would come from Cudlee Creek. Mother fancied she was a Salvationist—a good woman. It was likely she'd give Rina a home. But, until she came, how would Rina like to stay with us?

Rina's response was extreme. For a moment I feared she'd taken one of her turns. She threw herself at the hearth-rug and squirmed upon Mother's feet. She buried her face in the hem of Mother's skirt, then concentrated on the plaster rosette that marked the middle of the ceiling. "Oh, Mrs Hodge," she breathed, just the right degree of tremble in her voice, "how kind you are. What this means to me you will never know."

It was as good as the Tivoli panto: Mother and Meg stared, entranced. They might have applauded, had not Father returned with the doctor.

Rina charmed even him. He called her Brave little lady, and assured her there was nothing she could have done. Lizzie had fallen dead on account of her heart; she hadn't felt any pain, it was an easy way to go. He pronounced Rina in need of a dose of invalid port, and suggested she lie down to rest.

There was a spare bed in Meg's room, so Rina went in there. I felt like calling out a warning, telling Meg she'd better take care, but I knew it wouldn't do any good. Already, she'd fallen under her spell as much as everyone else.

Rina was clever, and switched character with chameleon-ease. When she'd lived with Lizzie, and wasn't being simple-minded, she'd cultivated a capable air. She'd shown an

interest in gardening and sweet-tooth cookery, had occasionally
dusted and swept. With me, she'd been more exotic. When I
thought of those Saturdays when I'd washed her hair I recalled
the Chinese shawl, the mole on her belly, the Egyptian Lounge
at Menzies' Hotel. Now, in the sanctuary of Meg's bedroom,
set about with hair-tidy and nightdress sachet, and a box for
hankies encrusted with shells, she was different again. Even
her body seemed to change. At Lizzie's I'd always been aware
of it. She'd flaunted it as she padded barefoot in the garden,
and bent her head over the basin of steaming water. But now, in
a borrowed nightie of Meg's, you'd never have reckoned those
interesting swellings were there—under the excesses of ruffles
and pin-tucks, the marching line of mother-of-pearl buttons.

She sat up in bed, her hair in two long plaits. It was hot outside, but in the bedroom it was cool. The curtains were drawn;
it was day-time but it might have been dusk. The darkness did
strange things to Rina's looks. Her cheeks hollowed out, her
face took on a pensive air. She was so beautiful, at the same
time so pathetic, that it would have been impossible for Meg
to have stayed aloof. Behind the bedroom door they became
girl friends, and my haughty big sister, who habitually exacted
servitude herself, was enslaved.

Mother thought it touching, seeing her serve a poor unfortunate so unselfishly, but it made me want to be sick. It was ridiculous, the things Meg did. You would have thought Rina to
be helpless ... the way she fed the fingers of toast, coddled the
spoonfuls of egg into her mouth ... how she carried up hot water in the china basin, and—careful not to slop—washed even
under her arms; then dabbed on lily of the valley talcum ... and
Rina lolling back, smiling while the stocking was guided along
her leg.

Teddy's picture-postcard of Love's Thermometer was
propped on the mantelpiece, but Meg appeared to forget him.

Rina was only with us for three or four days, but then, and
for some time after, home had a different flavour. I felt so bad

I might have been stranded in the nasty part of the cemetery. I disliked waking up, for her voice was the first thing I heard—coming low, insistent, through the wall.

Even Mother succumbed. Lunch grew more elaborate. Father raised his eyebrows, and said cold meat and chutney used to do. Now we had Marine Salad, which meant the cucumber shells were little boats, piled with pulp chopped fine (place-cards were attached to the bows of the boats as sails). The cheese was tinted pea-green with pistachio colouring, the hard-boiled eggs were sliced like water-lilies. We always finished with something sweet. It was curious how you could tire of meringues.

Rina paid Mother for the meals by acting the part of perfect listener. She sat on at table, dilating her nostrils in all the right places. She was particularly taken with the stories that featured Teddy and Meg. She spent a long time checking on Teddy's credentials. "Oh, decidedly," assured Mother. "Old Mr T. is rolling in cash. And there is class there, too, for he cultivates a superior type of apple; and, as well, there is Teddy's art."

Being girl friends meant you stood in front of the mirror for ages trying on clothes. And your bodies were always touching, for there were buttons to fasten and creases to coax away. And the effects were so successful or, alternatively, so hilarious that you must collapse on the bed ... clasping each other, laughing—though, really, it wasn't that funny. You were for ever linking arms and strolling under the fruit-trees. You usually carried a book of poems with a limp suede cover; you read the sad parts aloud, sharing alternate lines, and cried a bit because too much beauty hurt. There were creepy-crawlies in the grass, it was almost as hot as a heatwave: a lady was supposed to be lily-white, but you didn't care. It was thrilling to sun-bathe in your petticoats. Fancy, if anyone had seen.

I saw. It was home; I was friends with everything. The clothes-lines and the fowl-house, the roses and the daphne bush Mother worried over because it was sickly. But I crept

through the garden like a stranger; I went down low where the
fruit-trees began. The grass hardly swished as I pushed through
it. She wasn't my sister as she lay there next to Rina; their bodies
stretching out so still they might have been as dead as Lizzie.
It was Meg I hated most as, dreamlike, their mouths came
together.

10

Miss Rodda, though Lizzie's cousin, bore her no resemblance. She was a chatty little body in a strange squashed bonnet that reminded me, somehow, of a camera. After the funeral she sat with Mother drinking tea. She was Total Abstinence as well as Salvation Army, and had a stock of anecdotes that warned what one glass led to. She smiled joyously, as she told of blighted hopes and broken hearts; of Madge who took hot toddy as a cure for common cold, and ended up in the workhouse; of Tom who tippled at the Café Monico, and froze to death in the gutter.

Mother agreed the drink curse to be a terrible blight, and deemed it fortunate Father stuck to crystal waters. Then she guided conversation on to Rina Todd. Did Miss Rodda know her antecedents ... was she actually any relation? "Not that I mean to pry," she finished nicely. "But Rina's become like one of the family. We're all fond of her, especially Meg, and it's natural to wonder where she comes from."

For once Miss Rodda's flow of chat deserted her. She shook her head mournfully as she remarked that though dear Elizabeth was her cousin, and only lately deceased, it had to be said: she was a queer one. Eccentric. Odd. As much a recluse as the brute husband in Reverend McMurtry's *A Mother's Vision* (now that was a tale with a moral). She said, Would you believe it?—the first she'd heard mention of Rina was when she got the doctor's letter. Of course she'd offered to take the girl in; it was only her Christian duty. And though home was cosy, a veritable nest of comfort, it would be nicer still, the two of them together. And how thrilling to mould a life. She would introduce Rina to Band of Hope; bring her up to be sober and dependable.

Miss Rodda saw Rina as a little girl; she almost looked like one when she departed. I knew it to be impossible, but she seemed to have shrunk. Mother had sat up all night sewing her a dress to mourn in. She'd vowed it to be a perfect fit, but on the day Rina left us her body appeared lost inside it. Her eyes were red from crying; her hair was screwed up under a chip-straw hat. She looked so ugly blubbering into her hanky, that I began to think I'd made a mistake. Meg's kiss in the grass hadn't signified anything peculiar. Anyone might have pitied Rina and sought to console her. Probably it was a mistake, too, the time when she'd frightened me in Lizzie's dress. You had to make allowances for a loony. Though it wasn't always apparent, that was what Rina was. I felt better than I had all week. "Goodbye, goodbye," I called with the others, as Miss Rodda's trap set off for Cudlee Creek.

Things went back to being the same. Lunch was only cold meat and chutney, but I didn't mind. After a few days Meg stopped looking mournful. She sent away for a pair of Empire puffs, that turned out to be only ringlets attached to a comb; she resumed sighing over Teddy with Mother, and sharpened her pencils in readiness for the new term at the School of Design.

There was a plague of cockroaches in the kitchen, starlings were sighted in the orchard—they had a keen appreciation for every fruit. We began looking forward to Harvest Festival at church. The *Observer* played false with Little Leo Nankivell, who was supplanted by Miss Laurel Burns ... "Unconscious for hours—doctors baffled—sufferer for years—nervous wreck—in grand health today: DR. WILLIAMS' PINK PILLS".

One day there was an auction at Lizzie's. Everything was put in the garden, as if Rina was returned to indulge in a monster spring-clean. The bird in the glass case was revealed to be mangy; the crazy quilt dissolved at the touch.

It was the first time I'd been behind the squeaker hedge for years. I felt I betrayed Lizzie worse than ever by doing nothing as strangers trampled the flower-beds and fingered the apostle spoons. The auctioneer climbed on to one of the good bedroom chairs, and ran words together. It didn't take long for him to be done. Somehow the hoard of gold had been overlooked—there wasn't even the stick-pin crowned with a nugget to lend her status.

School started again.

Mr Kitto continued horrid, and plagued a new crop of little girls, but because he was part of the world of everyday, I was even glad to suffer him. Baby Pettigrew stayed quartered with the infants, but now Bully Edwards left him alone. Mercy had given him an admirer's cast-off Boomerang mouthorgan, and if you were Baby's friend you were allowed a blow.

School wasn't so bad, for I kept thinking that at the end of the year the inspector would sign a certificate—touch wood—that vouched I'd passed the Fifth Class Examination in Reading, Composition, Dictation, Drawing and Arithmetic. I would be thirteen and a scholar; a big girl, old enough to have done with learning.

Hilda Nutter was going on to the new high school in the city, but she was clever. She drew the snapdragon in freehand perfectly; her composition on the Death of Hector made you cry.

Hilda wanted to be a teacher. She was stout with greasy hair. She was mature: when she had her monthlies she stank.

Like Baby, she didn't get invited to birthday parties; her clothes were never in fashion. But sometimes I envied her. Hilda was strong. She wasn't scared to go where everything would be strange. She cared so much for learning she'd never be lonely.

Sometimes, when the Royal Reader was interesting and I couldn't wait to turn the page, or when Mr Kitto told of Good Queen Bess with her painted face, I even fancied learning more, myself. But then I thought of going away, leaving everything I loved: Mother and Father, Meg, the Hills—even Baby, and I knew I couldn't do it. It would hurt too much. I knew I was a coward, but all I wanted was to play at dutiful daughter.

The more the worry nagged that it was wrong to want only

that, the more stubborn I felt. Perhaps I matched Hilda in strength as I shut my mind to a life away from Fern Gully. I supposed I might turn into a maiden-lady like Miss Meek. I hoped so; it would be pleasant. I would grow hairs on my chin and have a habit of licking my lips; I'd wear my hanky in my sleeve and inspect it after I blew my nose. When a gentleman passed me in the street I'd blush.

Already the girls at school considered me curious because I preferred Baby to them, and wouldn't whisper stories behind the earth-closets, or say the rhyme that was rude. If they'd known of my spinster ambitions they'd have judged me as much a loony as Rina.

I didn't know why I was like that—wanting such a commonplace, yet singular life. I didn't know what had made me wary of abandoning childhood, of venturing from home.

When I thought about it I felt miserable, muddled up. Home was my favourite place, I wanted to stay there; but when I thought back to its beginnings—to the first bit of home I remembered, to the house at Prospect—I didn't only recall Chinky-Chinaman and rides on the tram. Now, home moved on into the Hills, I could still remember the nights when the voices quarrelling had frightened me. How I'd got into Meg's bed, and pushed myself close against her. She'd let me; she'd wiped away the tears. She said "Hush." That it wasn't them—not Mother and Father. Oh no. The voices were only part of the bad dream—they echoed on. "Go to sleep," crooned Meg. "It's all right." In the morning I'd usually forgotten the dream, I wondered why I shared Meg's bed. Why did I remember now, when Father's voice was permanently lowered, and Mother couldn't separate fact from fancy, and Meg hardly spoke to me any more?

11

It was during rest-break in artistic anatomy that Meg made friends with Miss Pixie Mott. Miss Mott was destined to be famous. She'd studied at Colarossi's in Paris; she had a studio as good as Teddy's; she was one of the New Women the newspaper warned of.

Miss Mott came to spend the weekend. She didn't disappoint. When you walked with her along the Gully Road everybody looked. She was peculiar, with her pale sharp face and inquisitive eyes; her hair cropped as short as a boy's, her mannish clothes.

Miss Mott talked in capital letters. The queer thing was, that where her appearance was austere, her words were decidedly sloppy. She was always on about Dame Nature and Burgeoning Spring, the Sacred Fire and the Immortals. She called Meg her dearest Rose-red, and wove a web of fairy-tales about her that reality couldn't snub.

When Miss Mott came to visit, Father was abed after one of his bouts. The house smelled of whisky and sick. Mother was all of a flutter—one minute nipping into the front room with the cobweb broom, the next flapping hopelessly at the kitchen window to chase away the tell-tale scent; then begging me to button her up. And, dear Heaven—she'd forgotten to empty the slops. And she had a suspicion the butter was off.

But the chops were frizzled to a nicety and the blancmange was deliciously slippery. And though Miss Mott's accent was flash, and she stared with her hard little eyes, her manners were bad. She put her elbows on the tablecloth, and picked up the chop bones with her fingers. You forgot to be scared, even though she had a private allowance, and was over thirty, and didn't wear stays. She talked such nonsense. Meg, she insisted, breakfasted off wild strawberries and washed her face with dewdrops and brushed her hair with dock leaves. "Beg pardon, I'm sure," apologized Father, passing through in a hurry to get to the lav. Mother blushed scarlet, but Miss Mott didn't turn a hair. She nodded her assent, and kept on talking. She said she was a Fatalist, sort of Greek. She'd love to have the old gods revived. So picturesque to kneel to Venus or Apollo.

Miss Mott came the next weekend, too; Meg stopped meeting Teddy in the lane. I wondered if he'd finished painting her portrait for the Autumn Exhibition at the Society of Arts.

Miss Mott's camp-stool was roomier than Teddy's—Meg was able to share it. She sat there, looking admiring, while her friend tinted moodily with her brush. Where Teddy's pictures were detailed, Miss Mott's were vague. They had titles like "Impression, Blue" or "Study, Pink". Teddy's pictures were drenched with sunlight; Miss Mott preferred to depict the elusive hour of dusk. Her moons throbbed with whiteness, her bushland was veiled in fog. She didn't think much of Teddy's efforts. He was content, she said, to merely mirror nature; she painted the Landscape's Soul.

Teddy's bedroom had silverpoint and a brazier, but Miss Mott could even better that. She had a tiny house in the city, all to herself. And she lived on anchovy paste and sardines, and dried her plates with a paint rag.

Teddy turned persistent. He showered Meg with postcards. As well as Love's Thermometer, the mantelpiece was ranged with actresses: Mrs Langtry in ostrich plumes, Mrs Forbes Robertson looking pensive. Next came the Royal photo bouquet, very stylish, which was a buttonhole with a photograph concealed. Meg got a pansy that might have been real. When she squeezed its stem an ingenious device caused the flower to tilt and reveal Teddy's profile. Mother said it was charming, and Meg couldn't help but agree. That weekend Miss Mott didn't come; Meg fastened the flower to her dress and wore it to church. That Sunday Mr Teakle nodded across the aisle, and in Tuesday's post came an invitation to take tea with him and Teddy.

She spent a long time getting ready. She wore the blue silk that matched her eyes. She pinned on the pansy. She walked in her old shoes along the Gully Road; I tagged behind with her best ones.

Just before the jam factory, we made the switch. I was supposed to go straight home, but I didn't. Instead, I pushed through the hole in the hedge and watched her walk down the slope. It didn't seem real that she approached Teddy's front door; that they were such old acquaintances he should greet her with a kiss.

Meg came home with sparkling eyes and a tin of choice fig jam. All her old enthusiasm for Teddy revived. When she mentioned Miss Mott her lip dismissed her with a curl. "Pixie paints well enough," she conceded, "but the poor dear will never reach Teddy's heights."

Packing-cases might serve as Miss Mott's grocery cupboard, she might be off to an inspired start on her gesso panel of Brunhilde in the Flames, but now—that rose-petal shower coming closer—she didn't matter in the least. Mother thought the wedding-veil should be simple, tra-la—single orange-blossoms on dotted net. And wasn't the new pyramid bouquet simply fetching?—roses, hyacinths, fine ferns.

Though Meg had to admit Mr Teakle's welcome hadn't been rapturous, he'd been kind enough. Perfectly civil. Though cold. And he'd complimented her on her colouring. But winced when she said where she'd gone to school. Wouldn't it have been dreadful if he'd known about Father and Bowden? And who was that ridiculous Miss Beck he kept bringing into the conversation?... Teddy at the wheel of her papa's De Dion, indeed; her mama's supper-table decorated with La France roses.

When she'd asked Teddy of Miss Beck afterwards, he'd taken pains to set her mind at rest. "A perfect bore," he'd assured.

"Hair of an aggressively red tone. No style." Though Mr Teak-le had winked, and declared her to have resembled a perfect dream, the night Teddy escorted her to the North Adelaide bachelors' dance. "Nobody of import," said Teddy firmly, and she'd loved him more than ever. Though he'd looked a bit confused. Hadn't met her eyes.

Miss Beck, however, was overshadowed by what happened next. Already it was April. Harvest Festival was over, Mr Kitto had organized a visit to the Autumn Show of the Royal Agricultural and Horticultural Society in the city. Teakle's had won several prizes, but what a pity Teddy hadn't finished Meg's picture for the Society of Arts—it would have been a double treat seeing that, as well. Easter came and went. Monster sharks were sighted at Port Lincoln; the Adelaide Skating Club held its opening meeting at the Glaciarium. Meg was excited, because one evening Teddy had promised to take her.

And Father began pruning the fruit-trees, and potting the tender plants. And Marshall's advertised winter fashions and novelties. It was lovely to have a fire again as you ate your tea; to swallow the last morsel of baked potato, and watch sparks fly from the Mallee root. Lucky Meg—skating to the sound of the string band would be a joy ... even if you only watched it wouldn't be cold, for hot water-pipes warmed each seat. In a minute washing-up would start, and tonight I'd be excused, for the history composition would take ages to write. But, really, I didn't care. Captain Collet Barker was a favourite. Poor old thing. It was mean of the blackfellows to murder him after his swim. But writing about it would be good. Sucking the new nib into prime condition—then tongue out for very best copper-plate. Holding your breath to make a nice thick downstroke; then a quick dash up, and commence the capital with a flourish.

I had just got the brave captain to Lake Alexandrina when everything was ruined. The ink blot looked awful on the page. Why did she knock so hard she gave me a fright?

"Who can it be?" asked Mother, wiping her hands on her apron. Then, changing her mind, she told Father to go to the door. You couldn't be too careful at night.

The voice sounded like Miss Rodda's, but as she came into view I started to wonder. The bonnet was on crooked, and the coat buttoned up wrong, and she walked with a little lurch. She looked so queer she might have been acting out the fatal effects of old pinky. Even her vocabulary was limited. She repeated the one question without pause.

"Is who here, dear?" asked Mother, sitting her down before the fire.

Miss Rodda shuddered. She spat the name out, as if it hurt her mouth.

Mother raised her eyebrows. Why should Rina be with us? We hadn't seen her since she'd removed to Cudlee Creek.

Saying Rina's name did Miss Rodda good. She unfroze. She cried a bit, but rallied to recover her chat.

Who would have thought the ungrateful minx would run off while her benefactress was distributing the *Temperance Record*?

Gone. And yet to master honeycomb stitch and bullion knot. And she never finished getting "What the Roses Say"—"Oh, welcome rain, and welcome dew, For water's best for me and you ..."—to heart. How could she leave the finger biscuits to burn?—and the chooks not fed and the dishes still stacking the sink. Flown. Who would have thought it? And leaving the front door wide open so next-door's dog got in and peed on the goat-skin rug. "And what I would like to know," finished Miss Rodda, "is where's my ring with the different coloured stones that spell out *Dearest* (diamond, emerald, amethyst, ruby, etcetera)? And the cameo that used to be Mama's? Not to mention the ten shillings gone from my purse."

Mother sucked in her cheeks. Meg said "Oh no."

"Oh yes, indeed," corrected Miss Rodda. "And I could go on to tell you more."

"Now, now," soothed Mother, keeping peace. "Go and put the

kettle on, Meg, there's a good girl ... Don't worry, Miss Rodda, Rina will turn up. She must have taken one of her fits. We'll find her. The wanderer will return, safe and sound and penitent."

Miss Rodda changed colour. "Return?" she shrieked. "Mrs Hodge, you do not know what you say. No. I shall not consent—I cannot. That girl shall never set foot in Rose Cot again. Why, if you but knew ... No, do not press me. I would die rather than breathe a word. Minx. Jezebel. No, Mrs Hodge, I beg of you. It is too disgusting to say."

Miss Rodda had to be put to bed. It was curious to reflect that she lay in Meg's room where Rina had rested before her.

In the morning the search began. The Gully buzzed with rumours. Rina had been seen moping over Lizzie's grave; trailing the Chinese shawl along the Gully Road; running at a jog-trot down the slope that led to Teakle's.

Which was where she was found. While Miss Rodda denounced her, Rina had been lying cosy in Mr Teakle's spare room. With the old man fussing over her as if she was a favoured guest. And Master Teddy fanning her brow and remarking he'd like to paint her as the Madonna. Mother got the facts next day, from Mr Teakle's housekeeper.

"But why go there?" asked Meg. "It's not as if she even knew them. Why not here, where she would have been welcome?"

Poor Rina. Though Doctor said she'd fled Rose Cot in a momentary delusion; though she begged Miss Rodda to believe her fingers hadn't been sticky—a thief must have crept in to snatch *Dearest* and cameo and ten shillings—the Salvationist refused to budge. "No never," she avowed. "Not under my roof."

People wondered what would become of Rina—the Protestant Refuge was predicted. Maybe Mr Teakle would have taken her on as a maid if the doctor hadn't had his brainwave.

"Of course," he exclaimed. "The very thing." Everyone had to agree: Gladwish House would be the perfect refuge; Miss de Mole, the perfect mentor.

12

Gladwish House hadn't always had its name; Miss de Mole wasn't always as you found her now. Once she'd been little Diosma, a flaxen-haired mite, her papa's pride, her mama's joy. And Gladwish House had been Violet Bank, one of the grandest houses in the Hills; a great stone mansion, its wide verandahs shaded by walls of clipped greenery, its gardens planted with countless varieties of shrubs and trees bearing the fruits of all climes. There was an orangery, a menagerie, and a flock of white peacocks. The estate was surrounded by an impenetrable hedge of prickly acacia; bronzewing pigeons and other game abounded.

Miss de Mole's father, Sir Harold, started life as plain Harry Mole, an errant younger son from Dorking, exiled from home to study Egyptology in Berlin. Such were his rose-bud good looks, rather than his proficiency in hieroglyphics, that the King of Prussia chose him to join an expedition to the ruins of the Nile Valley. But in the desert scandal occurred: Harry fled to England where he published his notorious *Notes From a Pocket Journal of Rambles Round a Lesser Pyramid* for private circulation. After a short spell in Bolivia, Brazil, he arrived at Port Adelaide; penniless, in 1851, his only possessions being a ring received from King Frederick before his disgrace and the head and wrappings of a mummy. The following year he visited the Victorian goldfields and amassed a considerable fortune. He appended the "de"; he settled at Fern Gully, and Violet Bank started to rise. In the sixties he married the relict of a late Congregational minister, and respectability was guaranteed. A munificent benefactor to religious and charitable institutions, his name became prominent in South Australian topography under villages, lakes, plains, and city streets. A son and heir was born, and Diosma the year after that. A knighthood was conferred. The future seemed assured.

When the Duke of Edinburgh visited Australia in 1867, Sir Harold entertained him. On his way to Lakes Albert and Alexandrina the Prince proceeded to Violet Bank where a sumptuous breakfast was provided. The estate proclaimed its loyalty with a host of floral arches; flags were suspended in unlikely places, and Diosma toddled forward with a bouquet. All the ladies present affected a limp, for it has been reported in the *Register* that Prince Alfred had a sore foot, and consequently it was considered the right thing to walk in a halting manner (in fact, Lady de Mole went to the length of having one heel of her shoes made shorter than the other). After breakfast the Prince went over the grounds and inspected the menagerie which included camels, kangaroos, wallabies, emus, native pheasants, and the peacocks. As he drove off for the Lakes, the ordinary folk of the Gully assembled at Violet Bank's gates to give him a cheer, and were allowed in to eat cake in a tent. In the evening a bonfire was lit, after which a display of fireworks finished the day's amusements, and further rousing cheers were given for both His Royal Highness and Sir Harold.

Such was Violet Bank's glory.

The next year tragedy struck. It was customary for the German Rifle Club to hold its annual Easter meeting on the estate, concluding the day's sport by serenading Sir Harold. In 1868, however, the programme was cut short—melodic part-song was notably absent from the proceedings. For little Tommy de Mole wandered from his nurse, and was accidentally hit with a bullet. He died in his father's arms.

Some blamed the tragedy on the peacocks: the feathers might be white, rather than coloured, but everyone knew them to be unlucky. Though it had been a particular pleasure of Tommy's to admire the dazzling arcs of silver as the birds turned in the sun, Sir Harold had all of them killed. Others said it was the fault of that heathen thing from Egypt. Accordingly, the mummy's head was presented to the Adelaide Institute.

If there was a curse, it still carried. Lady de Mole turned recluse; Sir Harold took to drink. It didn't take long for the remnants of his rose-bud charm to desert him.

Violet Bank's fortunes waned. Cash abounded, but spirit was conspicuously lacking.

Sir Harold—grown bloated, his face resembling a monstrous strawberry—consorted chiefly with the servants. Old gossip was revived, and updated with spicy additions. There was a stable-boy whom cook couldn't abide ... Fancy sighting him doing *that* under the lemon-tree with Master.

One October, Lady de Mole drowned herself in the fishpond. Only Diosma mourned her. Most others, including Sir Harold, seemed to have forgotten her existence.

When the Duke of Clarence and Prince George toured Australia in 1881 they participated in a kangaroo hunt, inspected Ned Kelly's armour, attended the opening of Adelaide's Art Gallery. Though they put in an appearance at Morialta House, on the western slopes of Mount Lofty, Violet Bank wasn't on their agenda.

By Sir Harold's demise in the nineties the estate retained little of its former grace. One by one the menagerie's inmates had wandered away (from time to time there were sightings of camels in the Hills). The grounds fell into neglect.

Most of the rooms were shut up; few of the servants remained. Yet Diosma lived on behind the hedge of prickly acacia.

Her piety was renowned. She rarely left the house, preferring to spend her time learning passages from her Bible, and conducting Protestant Sunday School in the attic.

Then the last de Mole was taken with a mysterious illness. Strange swellings broke out on her body; the irritation was terrible. All sorts of remedies were tried. Herbal doses gave way to blistering without avail.

The doctors gave her up, but Diosma's call home hadn't

come. The Lord had need of her to serve Him by suffering. She lingered on, singing hymns to prevent herself moaning, and one morning woke to find the Great Physician had answered her prayers. Though she could hardly move an inch, there was no more pain. She celebrated by changing Violet Bank's name and taking Sunday School from her couch.

And now years and years had passed and Diosma still lay abed. Turned into Miss de Mole; no longer young, still pious. Indeed, her virtue was such, that in religious circles throughout the nation, and even abroad, she was revered as approaching sainthood. Fellow-sufferers wrote requesting to be put on her Invalid Prayer List; missionaries in the field sent loving messages. Queen Alexandra expressed sympathy through the Countess of Outrim, as did Mrs Cook, authoress of *Rifted Clouds, or Light on the Weary Path*. Locally, it was considered lucky for brides to pop in after the wedding ceremony, to allow her the honour of first visit and a peep at the bridal attire.

The Rays, however, were Diosma's greatest achievement. It had all begun when one of the Sunday School scholars was found to be some months advanced in a certain condition. Cast from home, she appealed to her teacher to take her in. Baby hardly lived to breathe, but Winnie stayed on as general factotum; becoming the first of that company of unfortunates who sheltered under Gladwish House's roof, and were referred to by their protector as her Rays of Sunshine.

The house that, as Violet Bank, had offered hospitality to Royalty now sheltered a variety of misfortune. The worse the case, the more Miss de Mole rejoiced. She doted on addled brains and crippled bodies, blind eyes and shut-up ears. Humpbacks were a particular favourite. 1907, when Rina came, boasted a dwarf as gardener, and Old Cuff, who bettered even that, being so permanently hooped that his nose met his knees, and he was forced to venture forward, pocket-mirror in hand, that he might see what lay before him.

Rumour had it that if you were a Ray you dressed in only

the best (was it true that Pearl Biddle who'd once been a wash-
erwoman—till her arm had gone through the mangle—now
queened it in cherry silk?). And partook of giblet soup and roast
sucking-pig, tipsy cake and damson pie.

The only reason Doctor hadn't thought of Miss de Mole from
the start, was that to look at Rina you'd never have known anything was wrong. Most of the Rays of Sunshine displayed the
way the Lord had chosen to afflict them. Pearl lacked an arm,
Cook had a continual gurgling in her throat, Old Cuff patiently
bore his hoop ... the dwarf gardener ... last year's aged bearded
lady.

But Winnie, who'd sought shelter first, looked normal ...

Doctor went off to Gladwish House, and came back trium-
phant. The late bearded lady's place still hadn't been filled.
There'd been a club-foot enquiring, but Miss de Mole didn't
cater for Catholics. Rina, on the other hand, sounded perfect.
Already, Miss de Mole had composed her personal acrostic:

R est in Jesus, and wait patiently for Him.
I t is good to give thanks unto the Lord.
N one of us liveth to himself.
A cquaint thyself with God.

Miss de Mole was as good as the frog-bride or Rumpel-stilts-kin, but Mother's tongue never featured her. It seemed that a de Mole—even the last—should be treated with respect. When she heard I was to be one of the party that would take Rina to Gladwish House, Mother insisted I wear my best. She would have been horrified to have seen Teddy's buggy detour to pick up Baby Pettigrew on the way.

We were taking Rina to become a Ray of Sunshine; it was just like a holiday. Teddy was kind, and my sister's betrothed. He was nice to everyone. He treated me as a grown-up; didn't comment on Baby's unfortunate habit of sniffing; hardly differentiated in the degree of courtesy he extended to Meg and Rina.

Baby and I had the back seat to ourselves, while the others squeezed up in front. Duke, the horse, kept steady time, and after Rina was delivered we were off to have a picnic.

The sun was brilliant, though the autumn air tempered its heat. Teddy declared the day should be bottled and exported, to show people in duller climes the champion weather we produced.

Only Rina was a spoil-sport. Her lip stuck out sulky; she rarely spoke. Though Meg said wasn't she sweet, with her hair arranged in bands, she kept her distance. She squeezed more towards Teddy than Meg. You'd never have suspected them to be such girl friends as that kiss in the grass attested.

Rina was comely, I had to admit. Teddy had chosen her gown. It was a dull colour, but pretty; cut loose, and bordered with roses; as old-fashioned as her hair. Meg said she was dying to see what it looked like in the new painting. Miss Mott might have her Brunhildes in the Flames, her Lady Macbeths in Bed: Teddy had done Rina as the Virgin Mary.

Meg had never seemed so happy. She ignored Rina's sulks, and said the day was perfect. The sun, the sky; the weather generally. And so close to the two she liked best.

I supposed she had to say it, that it was only being polite. And Teddy was her love, and Rina her friend. But, in the back of the buggy, I felt hurt. She might have included me in the liking.

I wished we had reached Gladwish House. Duke was dropping manure something dreadful, and I was hungry. I wished Rina wasn't with us, though she provided the point of the drive.

She was so strange and otherworldly that, next to her, Meg's prettiness was mundane. I hoped Teddy didn't notice. But he was an artist, he measured with his eye.

We passed a garden full of chrysanthemums: the big white ones like snowballs, and Mrs Barclay, that was a beautiful mauve. Leaves fluttered down and I felt more miserable than ever.

The three of them sat in front like people in a play ... Meg's Goldilock curls under the straw she'd trimmed specially; Rina's rippling waves, the satin ribbon snaking amongst them (Teddy's hair was quite covered up by an artistic wide-brimmed hat). "Nearly there," he said as the acacia hedge started. I mistrusted him as much as Rina.

Something was wrong. There was a funny feeling. And all Meg could talk of was the fire-screen she'd begun in repoussé— the Sturt-pea motif would present a challenge. It was the way they never looked at each other, yet sat so close. He was "Mr Teakle" and she was "Miss Todd", but you sensed they knew each other well.

Baby and I waited in the garden while the others took Rina in. I felt disappointed. The house was impressive, certainly, with its wedding-cake façade; but plaster swags of grapes and excesses of cast-iron lacework couldn't compensate for what was lacking.

All the way in the buggy, as well as sensing atmospheres, I'd looked forward to something dismal: a lovely air of melancholy, signs of a general falling away. But though Violet Bank was Gladwish House, and Royalty didn't call, there was still money in the bank. Cash took the sting from death and disease; ensured the gravel on the driveway stayed ice-white as well as sharp. There was a lion's head door knocker, and a look-out tower topped with a flag-pole. But no cobwebs in the corners of the verandah, no splay-winged remnants of black and white butterflies, like there were at home. Miss de Mole might be inside, and the Rays of Sunshine, too, but the house was only ordinary.

The dwarf gardener did his job well enough. The buffalo-grass lawn wasn't allowed a bald patch; the hedge was nicely snipped. We wandered by a fishpond, and that must have been where she'd done it—poor Lady de Mole floating face down, her pockets weighed with stones, water-lilies tangling her ankles. But the gold-fish flickered through the shallows, the bronze angel-boy straddled his swan ... I couldn't summon up a single shiver.

Winnie had been bad enough to start with—living proof that a Ray didn't wear cherry silk. Rina was the only thing exotic. Winnie, all servile black and white, eyed the Madonna outfit, disapproving. She said Madam was expecting them, and then the door shut off my view.

But it started to get better the further you got from the house. Agapanthus ceased alternating with red-hot poker. Baby and I walked into a wilderness. Fennel was mixed with the Geraldton wax bushes; thistles outgrew the roses.

All the time we were pushing upwards. Past a stone dog with moss in his mouth, a Venus swathed with convolvulus. Then the last trace of garden disappeared. The earth was taken over by charlick and stinkweed. Then there was only grass, and the earth flattened out and dipped down—past almond-trees, oranges, lemons—to what was probably the Gully Road. Beyond the road were houses, very small. How strange to see Fern Gully become Lilliput.

We ran down the slope. Some of the trees were frilled with fungus; their boughs looked like ruffled sleeves. Others were smothered in creeper, mostly Japanese ivy, whose yellow flower smelled of old ladies—musky, nasty-nice.

The lemon-tree grew beside a creek that edged the road. The creepers had turned them into a series of leafy chambers, carpeted with soursobs.

Baby and I didn't speak—being there was too good. The lemons were little and hard. There were lilies by the creek, and some pink flowers I didn't know the name of.

We drove away from Gladwish House to picnic. Rina wasn't with us, but the funny feeling lingered on. Even Meg appeared to notice it. She stopped exclaiming over Miss de Mole—imagine doing fancy work and writing, holding needle and pencil between your teeth ... and what about when she said the poem of welcome: "I want to scatter sunshine all along the way. To cheer and bless and brighten every passing day ..."—didn't it make you want to cry? We jogged along in silence. The day was still fine, but now Teddy didn't admire it. The picnic was already ruined; I didn't raise an objection when Teddy unadventurously suggested we spread our tablecloth in the field below the Baptist Church.

Though I revived a bit when I tasted Mother's salmon patties. And Baby looked so ridiculous with the moustache of raspberry cordial staining his lip.

But we needn't have come: Mother needn't have insisted on a chaperone. For he didn't even take her hand. They sat with a lot of field between them, and filled the silence with Do you remembers.

"Do you remember," asked Teddy, "the earthquake of 1899?"

And she said she couldn't, and that gave him the chance to adjust the creases of his trousers, and tell how once—where we sat now—the oak-trees surrounded a pool of water where you were made into a Baptist. But because of the earthquake there was a stoppage of the spring, so the font was filled in to provide a suitable surface for tea-parties under the trees.

"Imagine", said Meg, and tried not to belch behind her glove. They might have been strangers.

You had to admire her persistence. She tried hard to save the day—carefully, yet oh so unconsciously, positioning her skirt so you saw an ankle; and worrying prettily over the speck of dust in her eye—Please would Teddy take a look? But nothing did any good. Though he took her elbow when they sauntered under the famous fourteen oaks, and she kept smiling as she matched him recollection for recollection.

"Do you remember at the Botanic Gardens in 1901 when the Duke and Duchess of York each planted a Chilean wine palm?"..."Well, no. Though I do recall when the old Queen died. All the statues in Victoria Square were draped in black."

14

Some good things were featured in the *Observer* but Mother said I wasn't to read. It was easy, though, to sneak a look when she went outside. The girl who ate a piece of cyanide in mistake for a lolly, and Baby Farming in Perth, and Muriel Knipe, the nine-year-old heiress, thrice kidnapped, were bad enough, but they couldn't compare with what happened to Maisie Hood.

How awful to be grown-up and married. Poor Meg, one day having to let Teddy do the beastly thing. But what about—even worse—when your belly swelled like a balloon and baby started to emerge? At night, sometimes, I lay in bed and worried. I couldn't stop the pictures inside my head. Sometimes I dreamed it happened to me. It was a relief to feel my stomach, flat as a board, when I awoke.

But what if you weren't even married? And still felt so sick, as if you'd eaten green almonds. Maisie Hood had.

Wicked Mrs Amanda Gay, who masqueraded as Madame Lenard, palmist, of Hindmarsh Square. And Maisie went in to have her fortune told, and the cards assured Madame she was in a particular state, and not from eating almonds. The bit that came next was the part I read fast, for the bad things that were good started happening, and Mother might come in before I finished ... How Maisie took the pills, and also a bottle of physic, and then Mrs Gay (Madame) applied an instrument, and sent Maisie off to walk round a bit, and then a mishap occurred ... How Detective Allchurch said that when he visited the accused she nipped down the passage and into the yard, and there was a noise as of something thrown among leaves. Detective searched the ivy diligently, and picked up three instruments and a bottle labelled "Extract of Ergot".

I couldn't stop reading, though I knew I'd feel dreadful after.
I did: I tore Maisie's page to pieces and put it down the lav. The
pictures grew worse in my head. I thought things about Mother
and Father. His underpants flapped on wash-day and I had to
look away.

There were two worlds that didn't meet: the rude one that
gave me the mixed up feeling; the proper, where people's bodies stayed covered. That world, this—which was real? The girls
said dirty things behind the earth-closets at school ... on Sunday the same mouths came open to render "We Are But Little
Children Weak" with a simper.

May wasn't much of a month; it rained a lot, and I took Bonning-
ton's Irish Moss for my cold. Miss Meek gave Mother a helpful
tip for removing mud spots—they disappeared in a trice if you
rubbed with raw potato. We got a new minister at church. The
old one went away after a farewell social in the Institute Hall,
where he was presented with a silver-mounted umbrella. But
Mr Kitto stayed on at school. Pinching the little girls, whacking
Baby; on Fridays imparting curious facts. Would you believe
that when a recruit joined the British Army his name had to be
entered sixty-two times in the various documents required by
the War Office?

May holidays began. My cough persisted, and I switched
from Irish Moss to Cherry Pectoral. I stood still for Mother
while she fitted my winter dress. She sucked on pins and considered my chest. I thought how horrid everything was: Maisie
Hood, and growing-up, and the cold sore on my lip.

The garden was drab and faded. The chrysanthemums
dragged in the mud, the asters were mildewed. The fruit-trees
looked ugly, their boughs bandaged against codlin-moth.

But sometimes there were mists and you could hear the jin-
gle of the horses' harnesses going down to Teakle's, though you
couldn't see them.

The pepper-tree berries turned so pale they were more white

than pink. Then they fell off. When it rained you trod on them, and there were rainbows on the ground.

The grass grew tall and thick; there were paddocks of soursobs. Even the natural world neatly divided in two. Summer—the hard red earth, seamed with cracks; the black snakes that coiled on the road ... winter—the stone-grey sky, the powder-green grass.

I wished I was one of the bulbs, growing in the earth in secret. Anything was able to hurt me. I had a suspicion that what had happened to Hilda Nutter wouldn't be long in coming to me. And what if, each month, I stank just as bad?

We went back to school and celebrated Empire Day. The occasion was marked by showers. In Adelaide the statues in Victoria Square were decorated florally. At Fern Gully we saluted the flag in the schoolyard, and dodged drips while the Chairman of the Board of Advice gave his address. A patriotic pamphlet was distributed, and Bully Edwards recited "Napoleon and the English Drummer Boy". The fife band played and we queued to receive currant buns.

During the breaks from lessons a series of games came regularly into fashion, and went out again.

In spring, humming gum-bubbles were all the rage. You peeled the fine rubbery skin from a new gum leaf and put it in your mouth to suck and blow—it gave off a lovely pop. If you put the skin behind your front teeth you could make it hum.

In summer, you got your mother to boil cherrystones. Some ended up white, some red. You carried them in a cheese-cloth bag with a draw-string, and used them to wager with.

The boys could hardly wait for the pittosporum flowers to appear. They provided perfect ammunition to aim through a shanghai.

Now, in winter, marbles were prized. Aggies—clear, with a spot of colour in the middle—were the best. Connies were coloured glass; some had cat's eyes, and were valued. Clayies, made of baked clay, were ordinary—commonohs.

The boys never played with the girls. Though Baby did, he didn't count. Poor Baby. His mouthorgan wasn't a novelty now. Bully's followers said cruel words; they reckoned he needed a dosing with brain food, and the attentions of the Marvel nit-comb.

Baby stood there and let them say it. He never answered back. His smile seemed to egg them on. Perhaps Mr Kitto was affected the same. One recess-time, after the whacks had sounded particularly fierce through the wall, we went behind one of the pepper-trees, and I took Baby's pants down to look. I hated Mr Kitto then. I seized Baby's hand and pulled him out of the yard. He started to whimper, because next lesson was handwork, and he was making a kettle-holder in tomboy stitch. It was a surprise for Mercy's birthday.

We took a while to get to Pettigrews', for, apart from Baby walking stiff, I kept making him halt for inspection: it would be a let down if the evidence faded. The last look outside his gate, however, was encouraging. The welts were revealed to be rosy; the skin was broken in two places, not merely one.

We marched the way the admirers went. Down the patch that skirted cabbage stalks and barbed wire, tomato sauce bottles and sick kittens, to end at Love and Mercy's door.

It was Mercy who opened it. Of the two she was my favourite. Love was so elegant she scared me. Even this early her coiffure was stabbed by a dragon-fly pin; her lips were blood-red, and she wore pearls by daylight, which Mother said a lady never did. But Mercy was beautifully frowsy. She smiled in welcome, and her mouth was no colour at all. You saw she had freckles; that there were sleep-dots in the corners of her eyes. Little bits of dry skin and powder and scurf seemed to float when she moved. She bent down and hugged me, and her breasts pressed together so hard the skin above them went wrinkly.

Their rooms were nicer than ever. Love had a new caller, a gentleman in sewing-machines, who'd given her a Wertheim that did three thousand stitches a minute. Mercy had added to her glory box with a tray-cloth embroidered in vine-leaf motif, a bead-work photo frame, and a hand-painted satin cosy. She was all of a flutter. The vine-leaf cloth had come from Ronald who worked in the Tourist Bureau. He had hinted at a summer excursion to New Zealand—the wonderland of the Pacific, Australia's playground and the world's sanatorium.

Love poured out glasses of restorative wine. We sipped, and wondered over Mercy's luck. Alpine scenery, only three and a half days' steam from the Commonwealth ... Te Aroha—where you took mud-baths and electric massage—with Ronald.

Mercy smiled dreamily, and reckoned things were looking up because of her brooch. Reg, in jewellery, had given it her only last month. Jasper set in silver was lucky, everyone knew. Likewise, hyacinth made you slumber, cornelian appeased anger, agate bequeathed eloquence ...

It was comforting being there. I drank with careful sips to make the perfect time last longer. My body felt drowsy, content. Mercy's skin was soft and white, with here and there bluish veins. Love's eyelids were greasy, and she had gold in her front tooth. The wine made me dizzy. Bees hummed in my head. The feeling went all over me; the zzzz was even in my legs. Hilda Nutter might come top in vulgar fractions, and know who said Kiss me, Hardy but I bet she'd never felt as good as this.

Then I remembered why we'd come. I shrugged free of the perfect moment and nudged Baby. He stood up and lowered his trousers.

"The swine," Love hissed, when I told Teacher had done it. "The filthy crook-back."

Mercy ran to fetch a jar of something soothing. The ointment went on Baby's bottom mixed with her tears.

She cried, but she was angry. She was all for setting off to school straight away. It didn't matter that she wore her kimono, that her face was still naked.

Love stroked her pearls and looked thoughtful. "Wait, sis," she mused. "There's a better way ..."

Her voice went soft, so I couldn't catch a word. But the idea must have been a good one, for Mercy started to laugh. "Ooh Love," she sniggered, "you are a comic. Ooh, what an idea ... Oh no, but I couldn't. Why, only to think of it makes me come over queer ... His hands—ooh, his hands are that long. Like a lady's ... And his back ... Ooh, Love. Oh no, I couldn't."

Love's voice was silky, persuasive: "My dear, admit it. You know it's the best way of all. Remember at the picnic how he gave you the eye—and more than that, too. I seen you, naughty girl, up to tricks by the sea wall." Idly, she scratched inside her blouse. "Why, it might even be fun ... think of it like that. And he's in pocket. And it'd be the best way to assure he kept his hands off Alfred."

Mercy chewed her lip. At last she gave a sigh. "Oh, all right, then. But I only do it for Alf, mind ... Poor lamb." She sighed again, and smoothed a crease from the vine-leaf tray-cloth and folded it away.

But soon she was giggling, and squeezed into her French corset. She appeared to be contemplating a visit. I saw the frizz between her legs, and it wasn't yellow like her hair.

Love helped Mercy get ready, all the time paying compliments: "Oh, my dear, that ribbon does wonders to your skin ... And your throat's that milky ... Oh, what a picture. The black silk with the rose-buds is just the thing."

Mercy admired herself in the mirror. She did look nice, though she wasn't the same person who'd opened the door. Her style was different, but she resembled Love. Now she didn't have a single freckle; her mouth was poppy-red, her finger-nails petal-pink with liquid rouge. The corset gave her another body. The loose powder and scurf were tidied away; she wasn't beautiful any more.

But she was pretty enough. It was a pleasure to watch her darting about, one minute smoothing her eyebrows with spit;

the next, increasing the décolletage of her neckline. Then a last
dab of scent and a twirl of her boa, and we were ready to be off.
For I was to be Mercy's escort. Baby would rest on a cushion
while I showed her the way to school. Mercy would give Mr Kitto wacko, and teach him to leave Little Brother alone.

Though it was winter and day-time, Mercy's outfit was more
suited to summer and night. Mother would have predicted she'd
catch her death with such a low neck, and only turkey-down to
snuggle up to. She had glass bangles up her arms and a velvet geranium on her hat. She tripped through the soursobs in
smart shoes.

But Mercy didn't appear to feel the cold. Her cheeks were
on fire, and it wasn't just rouge. The nearer we came to school,
the pinker she got. She held my hand but she seemed far away.
There was a funny shiny look about her. She could only take
small steps because of her skirt, but above waist she leaned forward as if to urge her legs on.

When we reached the picket fence she let go of my hand
and asked if there was lippy on her teeth. I waited while she
wiped the mud from her shoes. I started to worry. Ages had
gone by since Baby and I left at recess. It must be nearly lunch-
time—probably geography. We were doing North America, and
I couldn't get the Lakes to heart. So close to Superior, Huron—
what came next?—I was afraid. Oh dear (the St Lawrence is
navigable to the Rapids, near Montreal ... the Missouri rises in
the Rocky Mountains). He was sure to make me stand out the
front. His lips would curl back off his gums as the stick swished
air. I determined not to cry.

But when Mr Kitto answered Mercy's knock he didn't notice
me. He was that surprised to see her. I crept to my seat and pretended to concentrate on Eerie, Michigan, Ontario ... Everyone
else peeped too; even the pupil-teacher had a goosey-gander
from the infants' room. I could only see him from the back—he
had started swaying like he did when the hiding was going to
be a choice one.

Hudson, Delaware, Susquehanna ...

Mercy's tactics were a disappointment. She didn't shout or anything. She stood there fiddling with the tip of her boa, gazing at him as if he was God. It was queer. She was coming nearly out of her dress at the neck, and her face was painted, but at the same time she was like a little girl. Mr Kitto swayed harder; Bully Henderson smirked.

Love had been sure she would succeed. But Mr Kitto hadn't even invited Mercy in to keep warm by the fire. Though, when she said she must be going—Thanks ever so, ta-ta—he put Hilda Nutter in charge, while he escorted her across the yard. Bully stood up for a look out the window. He said old Kitto was showing her his thing by the pepper-trees.

Mercy had behaved so silly I didn't hold much hope for Baby staying unmolested (Lakes Utah, Chapala, Nicaragua ...). But Mr Kitto came back smiling. He said we'd all behaved so well he'd give us an early minute at going-home time.

When it was Arbor Day the Chairman of the District Council said it was the intention to make Fern Gully one of the prettiest nature spots in the state, and referred to the absence of a ground for the ladies' sports, and advocated a spirit of patriotism and a love of the Great Outdoors. The Chairman of the Board of Advice spoke on the destruction of trees in Palestine and how it had become a desert. Teacher said he hoped none of us children would ever be a George Washington and use the hatchet on the banana-tree the Chief Secretary had positioned last year. Then Baby Pettigrew was called out to plant a tamarisk by the water-tank (gums and acacias were planted, too, but Baby had the honour of first go). Then we marched to the Institute Hall where oranges, apples, lollies and biscuits were provided. Three cheers were given for the donors, and we were dismissed for a half-holiday. All the way home it was the only thing I could think of: how Mercy had worked a miracle ... Baby had turned into Teacher's pet.

15

A missionary came to church and told how thousands of high-caste Hindu children were secret Christians. They daren't tell the world, but in their homes they refrained from idol worship and were true followers of Christ.

Meg sang with the choir now. Her hat was one of the flashest, but it was a pity she sat up in front. She didn't seem as pretty as the girls on either side. Even Mother looked at her straight, and suggested a dose of tonic. Or the bones of white fish were supposed to be good, crushed and dissolved to jelly. But Meg said No thank you, and went to her room. She was always in there, now. Mother's mouth trembled. It was tea-time when she suggested the fish bones. She stared at Father across the cruet-stand. "Oh, George," she said (and I felt embarrassed, as if I was an eavesdropper—usually she only called him "Father" or the "Pup" that was short for "Papa"). Her voice was clear and childish, as if she'd woken from dreaming: "I can't understand. She never used to get the sulks. We used to make plans. The veil was to be dotted net. But now she never confides. And Teddy doesn't come to church. When was the last time she saw him?"

Meg mightn't smile, but things went on just the same.

The Governor unveiled new pictures at the Art Gallery—"Sunrise on the Cambrona Glacier", "The Foam Sprite". The Hog Bay Bachelors' Club met at Booleroo Centre. Mrs Honeywell gave a girls' tea-party in her beautiful house on Brougham Place.

At Fern Gully there was a week of intensely cold weather. The record frosts did injury to all plant life. Even the natural grasses were nipped. But soon it was spring, and the Hills were gay with blossom. Pink almond, then snowy pear and plum; and quince, cherry, apricot; finally apple.

You noticed things: the leaf of wild garlic was flat; wild onion had a hollow stem. African daisy was a noxious weed that once a year the prisoners were let out of gaol to pick—its petals were large; Jap daisy, though, was tame and small—you grew it in the garden.

The sun turned spiteful. It pretended to be mild, sickly. You sat too long outside, and didn't know you were sunburnt.

Rose-breasted galahs flew in the sky. I walked to the cemetery where Granma and Lizzie lay. Sheep droppings were everywhere.

At home, thunbergia, that Mother called golden glory, opened its hairy pods.

But best of all was the wattle. The pale silver sort didn't have much of a smell; the tiny gold one, with the pointed leaves, was sweetest of all. I sniffed and sniffed, but could never label the scent ... it reminded me of something—perhaps marzipan, but I couldn't exactly remember. It was pleasant, unpleasant ... I wanted to sneeze.

By the creek the kurrajong shimmered. The tree looked quite still; but when you came close you saw a constant quiver—the little leaves waggling. The shivery grass heads were like beads; the gorse came out, and the tea-tree. There were snowdrops and hyacinths, as well as flowers more strictly Australian. Pigeons cooed, and Mother had to call me twice to come in to tea. My monthlies started, and I hated being alive.

It was Eight Hours' Day and then Show Week. *Lady Madcap* opened at the Theatre Royal, and the *Observer* reported King Edward returned from Marienbad. We had more school holidays, and the weather continued so favourable that fungus diseases were rampant. Father thought up a new spray, a mixture of tobacco and soap: there'd be no scab or curl-leaf in our garden.

On Veterans' Day there was a reception for eight old men who'd served under General Havelock at the Relief of Lucknow. The Automobile Club held its opening run of the season, and Meg and I visited Rina.

This time there was no Teddy to escort us. We walked down the Gully Road. As we passed Teakle's Meg averted her head.

I was proud to show her a short cut. We went round the back way, by the creek. A plank bridge led to the trees covered in creeper.

Meg was panting as we climbed the slope. We stopped and gazed back at the Gully. "It's so small," she said. "It looks as if it doesn't matter."

Soon laurestinus and laurel replaced natural undergrowth. I picked stray twigs from Meg's hair, and she did the same for me.

Winnie let us in. She was a gloomy Ray of Sunshine. She led us upstairs, and my heart beat fast. Though Meg said Miss de Mole was all of a piece, I pictured her with bits cut off.

We entered the room, and she was merely a lady, rather pale, lying in bed. Her eyes were moist and doggy; her nose was droopy and soft. Her lips seemed unable to close on her teeth (probably it was all that gripping on pencils).

Straight away I knew I loved her. I felt queer inside, like I did when I saw Uncle Will's name on the obelisk. Miss de Mole was a saint. Her nightie was trimmed with best Irish lace.

We drew up chairs close to the bed and she started off on Dr Cuyler's rules for bringing sunshine into the soul: "Look at your mercies with both eyes, at your troubles with only one ..."

She spoke as if she was chewing flannel. I inspected the room.

The walls were covered with photographs. Fellow-sufferers and missionaries spreading Gospel seed jostled Queen Alexandra. There were silver-paper Bible verses and numerous knick-knacks. Miss de Mole saw me looking, and after "Keep your heart's window always open towards Heaven" she told of them.

The dollie pincushion was a dear, wasn't it?—it had come from one of her invalids. An evangelist, recently called from the harvest-field to rest with Jesus, had sent the Chinese card-case. The Lord's Prayer was carved on a cowrie shell; satin-stitch ravens succoured Elijah. Miss de Mole called the presents her love-tokens, and I longed to give her something, too.

Dear Miss de Mole. She had a phonograph, and a collection of Mr Ira D. Sankey's own records. Once, for twenty-nine months, she'd taken nourishment through a tube. Another time her brain was affected, and regularly she collapsed unconscious. Often Satan tempted her to give up the fight, and moan when the pain was severe.

I loved her. I saw myself flapping with palm-leaf fan and raising the cup of iced water to her lips ... I wondered how she went to the lav, and if she wore a rag each month.

But a handmaiden already existed. Miss de Mole declared Rina a model attendant. She brushed her hair with a good long downstroke and was a dab at reading aloud.

Just then Rina burst into the room, her face nuzzling a bunch of roses. She'd shed the Madonna look. Her striped bodice reminded me of a bumblebee.

She didn't appear to notice us. Her voice was cosy as she concentrated on the roses: Weren't they perfect pets? Dear Di must take a sniff ... up-sa-daisy, careful of thorns.

Released, Miss de Mole twitched on her pillow. There was pollen on her nose. I didn't love her as much.

Rina dropped the roses into a vase—but no, it wouldn't do ... Maybe the big glass one. There, that was better—didn't Diosma agree?

It wasn't till the vase was centred on the doily that she chose to see us.

Then she ran to Meg, all smiles. They were girl friends again. Miss de Mole's eyes were flat as she watched them touch cheeks.

Out on the landing Rina rolled her eyes. She didn't know how she survived. The bell rang for Morning Prayers at the stroke of eight ... She was sick of the stink of chamber-pots, and all that piping of hymns. Though didn't we think Diosma dressed her nice?—look, striped stockings.

Rina sauntered down the stairs as if Gladwish House was hers. She allowed us a peep in the drawing-room. We saw carved emu eggs and the silver trowel used by Sir Harold to lay the foundation-stone of the Gully Anglican Church. Rina smirked proprietorially as we admired the flower pictures made of birds' feathers, and the chandelier from the Paris Exposition.

We passed morning-room, breakfast-room, dining-room. None of them were ever used: a bullet felled little Tommy, and time stood still. Butler's pantry, china pantry, lavatory—the grand tour progressed. "Kitchen," announced Rina, and opened a door. The Rays were revealed at tea.

They were a drab bunch. The gardener might be miniature, but his moleskins were regulation cut. Pearl Biddle's stump was sheathed by a neatly-pinned sleeve. Cook gurgled, certainly, but it was a dolorous sound—you weren't entertained for long. There was a smell of burnt porridge. Winnie bit into a slice of tiger cake and watched us with narrow eyes.

I was glad to escape to the garden. Pansy circles and poppies existed, too. But Lady de Mole had drowned over there ... Why did the dwarf have a tab-cat beard—one side grey, the other black? Why was Winnie's underlip so sulky that the shadow beneath it looked like a scab?

Meg and Rina were a long way off on the lawn. Arm in arm, girls together. Meg was telling things. Why choose a loony as confidant?

I dragged my feet in the gravel. The *real* Violet Bank had been different ... There was a window, and she wrote her autograph with a diamond. The ladies wore lacy blouses to dinner. Silver candlesticks ... feeding the deer on windfall apples.

Gladwish House was a swindle. Miss de Mole and the Rays played cheats ... And then I saw him. He was bent like a hoop.

He walked as if he searched for threepence; the tassel of his cap whisking his nose; his pocket-mirror winking. One thing was true: Old Cuff.

He caught my reflection in the mirror and I went to meet him.

He wasn't surprised I should be there; I felt I'd known him for years. We walked slowly towards a trellis covered in vines. There were hardly any leaves yet; just a few curly tendrils. Beside the trellis was a bench. He eased himself down—poor Cuff. What was it like, always looking at the ground?

But once ... Lady de Mole was alive, though she had a different name; Harry ran round the pyramid. And Bob Cuff was eight years old, and set sail with Mama and Papa and Governor Hindmarsh in the *Buffalo*. They came round the horn, but he couldn't remember—only Rio de Janeiro, where Papa bought oranges and bananas. Holdfast Bay meant a house of reeds, and cockies screeching, and the blacks setting fire to the hills. On the Queen's birthday a bullock was roasted, and the blackies each got a white blanket—how comical they looked, lying wrapped up, with only their faces protruding ...

Cuff would remember, and then forget. Then start off again, and now he was older (but still young), and lived at Fern Gully.

... The cows all had flower names. Daisy was a Friesian with a sizely udder, it hung down so long she tripped on the teat. But horses were better than cows, so Bob began driving the coach. He was courteous to all, exceedingly attentive to lady passengers and children, a true expert with the ribbons. But that couldn't help him when the dog ran out at the cutting: the horses swerved, Bob came unseated, and was crushed between cliff and coach. And turned into Old Cuff.

Who sat beside me now, and smiled. Tragedy wasn't so bad; you had to put up with something. It could have been worse ... Governor Musgrave married a beautiful American, niece of Cyrus Field of Atlantic cable fame. But that didn't stop Harriet Joyce, their petted darling, taking a tumble into the bath of

scalding water, and being mourned by a Cathedral window and
a box-tomb. Horrid things happened—life was like that, chuck-
led Old Cuff.

Sitting in the sun, his voice was reassuring as it sorted
through a grisly repertoire: the female Father Christmas whose
cotton-wool beard caught fire when the candle toppled from the
pine-tree; the young blood in Sydney, bemused at full moon,
who pierced his breast with a hat-pin and swam out to sea (another hat-pin one was in America, when the gentleman hugged
his sweetheart so tight he ended up impaled). You could slip on
an icicle and be dashed to pieces at the bottom of the Katoomba
Falls; you could choke on a piece of dumpling. Old Cuff reckoned he and Miss de Mole had enjoyed lucky escapes. Any one
of those things might have happened.

The most dismal fate, surely, was to end up nothing at all;
determinedly neither one thing or another; any evidence of the
peculiar cold-shouldered.

That was what was wrong with the other Rays. They didn't
know their luck: Cook gurgled, Gardener didn't grow, Pearl
lacked an elbow, and Winnie a reputation; but because they
disowned them, their afflictions were worthless.

Cuff treated his back with respect and was rewarded. Only
Lizzie, pushing her perambulator, brewing her remedies for
sickness, had been as dignified, as beautiful.

I was glad we'd visited Gladwish House.

I'd met Miss de Mole, and for part of the time she hadn't disappointed. Only when Rina appeared had Jesus ceased being
her friend, and she'd lain in bed diminished, merely an invalid
I pitied.

And I'd made acquaintance with Cuff.

And on the way home Meg's mood was considerably lighter.
She remarked on the flowers by the wayside and the fact that
spring had come. From time to time she felt in her pocket, as if
it held a lucky charm. Once she drew out a slip of paper—she

read what was on it so tenderly, it might have been a love note from Teddy.

When she saw me looking the paper returned to her pocket. But not before I'd read the first line. It was only a name. I wondered who Madame Mora was.

16

It was lucky Meg didn't care for Teddy because the newspaper announced his engagement. Miss Beck and her papa's De Dion and her mama's La France roses had got him. There was dancing at The Gables, Walkerville; the supper-table was decorated with violets and daffodils, the icing of the dainty cakes being either heliotrope or yellow to match.

It was Mother who took it badly. All day she lay on the bed with the blind pulled down, though it was lovely out. Father urged her to buck up, without avail. "The shame of it," she moaned. "What will people think?" She kept reciting bits of Lady Kitty's report aloud—"Miss Honeywell, azure; Miss Dew, sequins on décolletage; Miss Cowell, white glacé ..."—in between berating the name of Teakle.

But Mother only lay in the dark for a day. Next morning she was right as rain.

Every cloud had a silver lining.

It was Providence, really ...

The Beck girl would rue it, for sure. Meg was well out of his clutches—the snake in the grass, the chinless wonder.

Besides, there were other fish in the sea. Only last week the young men of the district had decided to form a Mutual Improvement Society. They'd meet in the Institute Hall on alternate Mondays to debate "Does Australia devote too much attention to sport?" and "Should the state have a monopoly of the liquor traffic?". There'd be readings from the Poets; a nice type of person would attend.

Mother lowered her sights and moistened her lips. This time the story would stay modest ... The butcher's son was pleasant enough—he handled the knives with quicksilver fingers, he wielded the chopper with ease. A lovely lad, in fact. Did Meg fancy rump steak for tea? What about popping down and getting some? Though it might be an idea to change into Swiss muslin first.

But Meg stayed faithful to her old serge skirt. Though she hadn't cried like Mother, and never mentioned Teddy's name, you could tell she had a Sorrow. Swiss muslin and Feather Shop necklet hadn't enjoyed an airing for ages. "To put it plainly," Mother mourned, "the girl has lost her style."

Heroes abounded: the butcher's son; Bully Edwards' big brother who served as lanternist when Reverend showed slides of Palestine ... What was lacking was a heroine. Spoil-sport Meg wouldn't play. She had turned colourless. She didn't say a word, now, when Father chewed Yankee plug.

But one day Meg came home from the School of Design looking almost excited. A pink spot burned on her cheek. She said she had a favour to beg. If Mother wished to give her a treat, please might she holiday in the city? Miss Mott had a house all to herself; there was room for Meg, and Pixie had offered. Oh Please. If Mother loved her she wouldn't refuse.

Though Mother pulled in her lip at mention of Miss Mott, she was amenable enough. She saw no reason why not. Meg could relax and fit in some shopping. But she would have to ask Father, too.

Curiously, it was he who seemed determined to thwart her. He made Adelaide sound as wicked as Melbourne. The School of Design was all right for the day-time, but things were different at night. Miss Mott's voice might be lah-di-dah, but a New Woman wasn't a lady. He didn't care for her—puffing at cigarettes, cutting off her hair.

Meg faced him coldly and stopped playing fair.

Very well, then. If he wouldn't trust her with Pixie, alone, Thea should come as chaperone.

I darted forward. Suddenly, it was the thing I wanted most

in the world. Father had to agree. "Oh please," I cried. I never
went anywhere. It was always another who saw the Hereford
bull and the Shropshire ram at the Royal Show. I'd missed out
on *The Story of the Kelly Gang* by Biograph, and Darkie, the ed-
ucated horse, in Fenton's Circus.

Mother's bodice rose and fell. We were an army against
him. He sat before us in his work boots that were only used
for gardening, his silly useless fingers drumming on the almanac. I hated him, I knew Mother and Meg felt the same. The
room shrunk small. We pressed together, and yet we seemed
to fill it. I wanted to scream or break the china vase shaped
like a swan. They were both ruined—Mother and Meg. No
real dreaming left. Mother's eyes bleak as she started another
story she didn't believe in ... and she bought the hat in secret,
and her mouth flinched when he looked at the label and said
it was too expensive. And it was her money, though it came
from his wallet; he'd never lifted a finger to earn it ... And once
Meg had been pretty as a princess, a queen. But it hadn't last-
ed long. Teddy had done it. And I hated them—men. They
wouldn't catch me. I would run and run. I might even have to
run out of the Gully.

He sat there. He was no one, nothing, though we'd had to
take his name. He only came from Bowden, a suburb of smoky
aspect.

Father lowered his eyes. Meg's cheek burned brighter as she
pressed her advantage. She had it worked out. It would only be
for next weekend. We'd leave in the coach on Friday, and come
back on Monday morning.

Father still looked surly, Meg was trembling. At last Mother had inspiration. Now her bodice had slowed down, and her
voice was moo-cow calm. "Oh do say yes, Pup. Besides, it will be
educational for Thea, something to remember ..." Saturday was
the celebration of the Jubilee of the Botanic Gardens—there'd
be a moonlight assembly in the grounds. Where was his sense
of history? It would be thrilling for the girls to attend.

Father relented, and I felt proud. For once I had been able to help her.

I squeezed Meg's fingers, but she didn't smile in return. She had beaten Father, but she looked as if she wanted to cry.

17

I was with Meg at Miss Mott's; I slept on a couch in a real artist's studio. Propped against the walls were canvasses: ladies
with goitres watched me undress. There was a delicious stink
of turpentine and oil-paint, even though the window was open.
Tacked to the walls were reproductions from the picture gal-
leries of Europe—in the half-light of early morning I surveyed
countless angel wings.

The house had character; you could tell someone different
lived there. At the moment Miss Mott was enamoured of native
flora. There were stencilled friezes of gum leaves in every room;
the cosy-cover was appliquéd with waratahs, the tablecloth
with Austral bluebells.

I hadn't imagined Miss Mott would stoop to a cosy or a cloth.
But they were there; and at home she kept her elbows off the
table, and tapped her cigarette ash into a saucer. The bit about
her living on anchovy paste wasn't true, either. Tea had been
cold collation; and Miss Mott shredded her lettuce into mer-
maid's hair, like Mother. That was disappointing, but the part
that made me lie awake and worry when I should have been
sleeping, had started in Victoria Square. I'd climbed from the
coach after Meg, and Miss Mott's eyebrows had flown so high
they'd almost touched her jaunty straw brim.

"My God," she cried, hyperbole deserting her. "I never reckoned on you bringing the kid."

They walked down the street ahead of me, as if three was a
crowd. Miss Mott courted Meg with little attentions—guided
her elbow along the pavement, whispered into her ear. I felt
so abandoned that I was able to examine them coldly, as if
they were strangers. Meg had put on weight. Though her stays

were pulled in tight, her hips looked big.

Miss Mott fussed so much you'd have thought Meg to be an invalid, as sick as Miss de Mole. But she did walk peculiar ... as if her body didn't belong to her, as if she walked in her sleep. I tried to remember her before—before what? All I could date from was Teddy. Before him, Meg had been skinny and neat as a pin. She'd treated her body as if it was precious; even jabbing at the moons on her fingernails with reverence.

We reached the house. Though it was in the city, a stone's throw from Rundle Street and King William, it had a picket fence and a creeper. I admired frieze and cosy and tablecloth. It was decided that Meg would share with Pixie; I could have the studio couch. After tea they talked; but it wasn't a proper conversation, they might have been telling riddles. Most of Miss Mott's sentences lacked endings. Her voice trailed off, and her eyebrows took over the action. I was tired of her smirks and side-glances; when she suggested I might explore the back yard I was glad to go. But you couldn't give much attention to a few geraniums and a rose succumbing to mildew ... Inside again— alone in the studio, while, next door, they whispered on—there was a portfolio of chalk drawings: more bee-stung lips and elongated necks. Then an album of Cathedral views, and a book I found under the couch. Queer, that Miss Mott should take an interest in Feminine Hygiene. Douches and diagrams of funny things, like rubber thimbles.

They sent me early to bed. I lay in the dark, indignant, trying to make sense of the shadows. There was a chink of light under the door, but I kept thinking of sinister things. I rose, and took revenge by peeing in Miss Mott's Benares vase.

Back in bed, I felt nicely melancholy. My life seemed hopeless. I couldn't do knob stitch in knitting; I didn't have a Russian blouse. My father was common, and sometimes when Mother stopped telling stories she threatened to drink disinfectant.

When I slept Teddy and Rina crept into the dream. Meg was there, too. It was important, I had to warn her. Teddy was

nothing—I saw him pick his nose and roll it. Rina was the one
to watch. She wanted Meg to go on a picnic. "No, no," I called.
"Don't stir your tea with a twig of oleander."

I woke up. It took ages for morning to come, and the angels'
wings to be revealed.

After breakfast we set off to explore the city.

I hadn't thought Miss Mott would always be with us, a faithful shadow, pawing Meg's arm. I'd imagined us strolling off
alone—just the two of us together.

In the Hills it had promised to be an adventure ... Miss Siam,
the elephant, once queened it in the Zoo, now she stood stuffed
in the Museum. And over there was the Torrens Lake where
you could ride in a motor-launch or cross the bridge to North
Adelaide, where the élite had splendid mansions. You could
climb to the top of the Post Office tower; or go further afield to a
watering-place: Largs Bay, the Semaphore, Glenelg.

Reality was different. Meg still wore her old skirt, and her
steps were laggard. She didn't appear to notice anything, not
even the shop window dummies.

We walked down Rundle Street. All about us people were
having fun—eating lamingtons and frog cakes in tea-rooms;
admiring engagement-rings and Balmoral boots. I knew they
didn't want me with them. Now they were walking slower;
now we had come to a halt. And Meg was feeling in her purse,
and Miss Mott was being sarcastic. "How do you fancy a short
cut to Switzerland?" quizzed her brittle voice. The collar of
her shirt-blouse was so tight it bit into her neck; her mouth
was smelly from cigarettes. And then I saw it wasn't a joke—
we had stopped outside a sign: THE SCENIC WONDERS
OF SWITZERLAND, and adults went in for sixpence; it was
threepence if you were a child. Meg pressed a coin into my
hand. She said she and Pixie had business they must attend to.
I would entertain myself on the observation train (careful not
to sit by a man), and then take a peep into one or two shops.

We would meet on the Beehive Corner at noon.

I nodded, and managed a smile. They waved tata, and the quill on Miss Mott's sailor-model bobbed away.

She was my enemy: I could play just as unfair.

I kept behind a lady with a parasol. Following them, I felt better. They wouldn't trick me; Switzerland could wait. I was Hiawatha creeping through the forest ... Now it was Hindley Street, not Rundle, and Miss Mott's feather stayed in sight. They swerved down a side street but couldn't shake me off. I came out into North Terrace.

The Terrace usually meant culture; its nickname was Educational Square. The Botanic Gardens were up one end; Government House was the other. In between were Institute and Reading Room, Art Gallery and University. But I had come out opposite the Railway Station. Though Parliament House was over there, too—and up from that the Boer War horseman who pranced for Uncle Will—this part of the Terrace was foreign. There were hotels and coffee palaces. A girl nearly swung into me, and Mother would have called her fast.

Miss Mott's hat hurried ahead. Then it came to a halt. I peered from a doorway, and couldn't believe my eyes. For now there were three figures, not two: Meg and Miss Mott had been joined by Teddy Teakle.

I stopped being cautious and ran down the street. I was sure it had been *here* I'd seen them—there were steps, and then a door and a row of bells. Beside the bells were several fly-specked cards: W. Kelly, high-class American dentist; Madame Mora, the only Yorkshire palmist ...

That had been the name on Meg's piece of paper—coming back from Gladwish House she'd treated it like a lucky charm. Rina knew about reading tealeaves; I was sure she'd given Meg Madame's name.

But why did Meg want to have her fortune told, why here? It was a dirty looking building, most of the blinds were drawn. I wouldn't have gone to that dentist for anything in the world.

And if she had to pick a palmist, why couldn't she have tried one well known? Every week in the Miscellaneous column there was a list of good ones: Professor Kennedy and Madame Phyllis, King and Queen of Astrologists; Zingara, mental scientist (magic bowl)... and the King and Queen were opposite the Trades Hall, Zingara next to St Paul's Parsonage—surely that guaranteed respectability?

Then, for no reason at all, another name came into my head: *Madame Lenard*. And I couldn't, I wouldn't remember—but I did. Madame Lenard was wicked Mrs Amanda Gay who applied an instrument to Maisie Hood. I started running back along the Terrace. Towards the clean Kapunda marble of Parliament House and the Boer War statue.

People were staring, but I didn't care. Outside Government House was a jacaranda-tree. Blue petals were floating down, and high on the flag-pole the Union Jack waved. My uncle was a hero, killed in the War, but I felt I'd never be safe. There were dog turds in the gutter, and a man spat a blob of phlegm. The newspaper world had suddenly become the real one. But no— she was my sister. And Teddy had his name on the jam tin; he wore flannel trousers and an Old Boys' tie.

I reached frog cakes and engagement-rings and the short-cut to Switzerland. A porter whose gloves were as spotless as Teddy's trousers stood by a potted palm. I queued at the ticket office and paid my threepence. I was transported across the world. We hurtled over viaducts and through tunnels at the apparent rate of seventy miles an hour; the Jungfrau was neatly labelled ... and all the time I was back there, standing at the door. The card said "Madame Mora". Teddy had been there, too. Oh Meg. I was still crying when the train stopped and the lights were turned up, and the stately porter announced Rundle Street.

18

But they were on the Beehive Corner at twelve o'clock, precisely. And Meg looked just the same—perhaps even a little brighter. I began to think my eyes had played a trick. Teddy seemed as much an illusion as Switzerland.

Back at Miss Mott's, Meg couldn't have been nicer. We sat in the yard, and she combed my hair and said its colour was improving. And I had bone-structure, and next year, when I'd left school, good things would happen. We'd go for a holiday to Port Victor; take the excursion tram to Granite Island and eat ice-cream in the sun. She was my sister again, not someone unknown. Till Miss Mott called from the door that she should come in and rest. Meg was swept away, and I was left with the mildewed rose.

I thought about Miss Mott—why I didn't like her. At Fern Gully she'd been a novelty ... jabbing with her paint-brush; wasting all that spit on the twin causes of Meg and Art. But now, though she still talked in Capitals, her sentiment wasn't the same. She cared just as much about Art, but with regard to Meg something had changed. She was still Rose-red, but Miss Mott pronounced the name different. Bossy, rather than cooing. She was always doing little services, but her eyes were harder than ever.

Miss Mott was a queer one. She dressed like a man, except for the trousers, but read up on rubber thimbles. I hated ladies with sandy lashes and pale lips. What made it worse were her fingers. She was always rubbing in hand cream, lavishing them with every care. It was unnatural to buff up your nails when you didn't bother with powder.

Lunch was tomato sandwiches. Meg kept lying on the bed. It

didn't mean anything. Everyone got a headache.

Tea was meat pies out of a paper-bag. I felt a stirring of interest. Perhaps tomorrow would mean anchovy paste.

Miss Mott sat opposite, very stiff. Sometimes she frowned, as if she had a problem. She didn't look at me once. I watched the hands of her fob-watch slip round, and wondered when we'd set out for the Gardens.

Now she'd started an attack of the fidgets. Crumbling the last of her pie, fiddling with her fork ... She jumped up and ran into the bedroom. I hoped Meg hadn't forgotten the moonlight assembly.

I went to change my dress. I'd just put my coat on when I heard them having a row.

At first it was mostly Miss Mott. You'd never have thought her a Fatalist. "It's absurd," she cried. "I won't take the responsibility ..."

I pressed my ear to the door.

Meg was laughing. Then it sounded as if she said, "Can't you understand? It isn't going to happen—it hasn't worked."

They went back into the room, and I couldn't hear. I admired myself in the mirror. It was true: I was improving. My hair had goldy lights, my eyes were as blue as blue ...

If I held my breath till I counted to twenty, things would be all right. But I didn't care—it didn't mean anything. Pixie Mott was a cockroach.

There were footsteps in the passage, and Meg came into the studio. She was pretty again. She'd pinned a bunch of violets to her collar. Her eyes were sparkling through her veil.

Miss Mott came out of the bedroom, pulling on her coat. She was that thick-skinned. We didn't want her, but she wouldn't be shaken off.

The trees along the Terrace were lacy; through them you could see stars. Queen Moon smiled down, and Adelaide was the Holy City—born free, without convict birth stain.

We went through the gates to the Gardens. It was romantic, a real Continental. The paths were densely packed, everyone wore their best. The Locomotive Band played on the lawn by the fountain; the United Labour Party one was by the tennis courts.

All the green-houses and hot-houses were illuminated. We admired pelargoniums and orchids by Vauxhall lamp. It didn't matter that Miss Mott jumped out from behind the Victoria Regia lily; that she tagged us down the avenue of Moreton Bay figs. There were ponds and willow-fringed lakelets. And Niobe, Venus, the Four Seasons. In the Rosary was the Amazon group in bronze, secured by private subscription from the Great Exhibition in London.

Mr Holtze, the curator, was famous. There was an artistic tea-kiosk, and the lilies formed the finest collection in the southern hemisphere. In the beginning there'd been merely gum-trees of patriarchal age. The pioneers took the trouble to remove them, and now the Botanic Park was the Rotten Row of Adelaide, with miles of winding carriage-road through avenues of tender green.

Once there'd been animal cages in the Gardens; now the Zoo was separate—across the lake I heard a lion roar. To the east was the old Lunatic Asylum. In the Museum of Economic Botany was a showcase of poisonous plants: herb Paris and hellebore in saucers.

We stood on the lawn. Before us was a miniature Crystal Palace. All round it were giant knobs and needles. Meg held my hand, but I pulled back. She asked what was wrong, and the lion's voice faded away. We walked towards the Palm-house by way of the Rock Garden.

There was a cactus in a pot on the window-sill at home; these were only bigger. But I hated their prickly fleshiness, even though dew-flowers bloomed underneath. They stood so still, they leaned queerly. The Palm-house might be hung with Japanese lanterns (... and oh, wasn't the fern grotto pretty, cried Meg), but there were shadows.

I was lost in a jungle of stems. The glass walls didn't shimmer, they were clouded with slime. There was a sound of creeks gushing, oozing.

If you wore spectacles you had to take them off—the heat fogged them up. A man like a blind man bumped against me. Some of the ferns were yellow at the edges. I couldn't breathe; my nose felt plugged with moss.

Then I saw Meg, and as I pushed towards her she jerked forward again. Her face was pale; she was holding her stomach. It was happening, just as I knew it would.

Miss Mott reached her before me. "Take her other arm," she hissed, and we were dragging her down the path.

She started to walk. Jerky, bent over.

A bell was ringing; everyone was going home. At the gates the crush was bad and people were scaling the fence.

But we were out in the street, and Miss Mott was urging her on.

She lay on the bed. Miss Mott's waterproof was over the sheet. Already the towel between her legs was stained.

I wiped her face with the flannel. We were alone. Miss Mott had gone for the doctor.

She bit her mouth and I prayed they would hurry. "I didn't think it would work," she said. "In the end I didn't want it to."

She was my sister, but God had let it happen. Adelaide kept a Puritan Sunday; there was a Vigilance Committee to guard the young men's morals, but they hadn't been able to stop this. The baby bled away, and I loved her more than ever.

Doctor was little and grubby. He looked sideways out of his eyes; his moustache was yellow at the edges like the dying fern.

He frowned when he saw me, and they made me go into the studio. I sat on the couch with my knees pressed together. I felt it was happening to me.

19

And because I loved her I went back to the Gully on Monday morning, and smiled, and turned it into a joke: naughty Meg, succumbing to the lure of city lights—off to Mrs Bosley Jenkins' evening at the Lyric Club, where the death act from *Camille* would be done in a fluffy wrapper ... The Rose Show at the Exhibition Building ... Mrs Tolley's tea, where a roulette wheel was promised, and everyone would feel rakish as they queued for a spin.

Oh no, Meg couldn't come home—not yet.

Mother clasped her hands and cried that her girlie was on the mend.

"Come on, Pup—smile ... Well, yes, she's disobeyed your orders by staying a few extra days, but these are important years."

Mother hoped Meg would take advantage of Miss Hewer's toilet salon in Commercial Bank Chambers (a face-steam was the latest thing), and return to the Gully refreshed. The butcher's son wouldn't wait for ever.

I went to school. I learned. That St John the Evangelist wrote Revelation on the island of Patmos. That the Egyptians prepared a rush called papyrus, whence the word "paper" was derived. Mr Kitto fixed his mouth in a terrible grin, and told of explorers penetrating the interior. Mr Eyre lived on dried horseflesh, eaten raw. Captain Sturt crossed the Stony Desert where the heat was intense, causing the ink to dry on the pen, and the fingernails to break like glass. The pepper-trees whispered outside the schoolroom; a blowfly buzzed at the pane. But that world wasn't true. There was always another layer. Teddy sent the picture-postcard of Love's Thermometer, but was engaged to marry Miss Beck. Meg sang in church, but lay on the bed while the strange doctor rolled his sleeves.

History was best of all. There were names: Anxious Bay, Mount Misery, Cape Catastrophe.

I waited for her to come home; my body felt cold inside. The apricot leaves were heart-shaped, and between them were beginnings of fruit. But at night I stared into the darkness. It didn't matter if you had a hero uncle. Or got the wish-bone when it was chicken for tea. Or never walked on a crack. The black trap could still fall; the coldness creep upon you.

But on Tuesday and Wednesday mornings came a reprieve. A sandy ocean stretched in distressing monotony before them. There was neither grass nor water, and no alternative but death or a final retreat.

Explorers weren't ordinary. Their mouths didn't snigger secrets; their eyes didn't judge you up and down. They were no relation—Mother couldn't talk the mystery away, and turn them into baby brother Willy, who had a stammer, and ran when the big dog barked. Explorers didn't care about Meg; they had other things to think of. They left the banquet at Government House and marched into the wilderness with silken Union Jacks.

Bourke and Wills eating nardoo seeds and burying their journal in the sand, and ending up as statues in one of the principal thoroughfares of Melbourne. Kennedy in Queensland, hedgehog-bristled with spears. Bass and Flinders, in the little boat *Tom Thumb*, looking for rivers ...

Teacher read on, and a new thought came into my head. I would pass the exam and get the Fifth Class Certificate, and not just stay in the Hills. But be as good as Hilda Nutter, and go to the high school. Lead a different life, be another person.

I would be brave enough. I'd give up Mother's scones and breakfast in bed. And the sure reward of growing up twin to Miss Meek, with a cardigan that hid the chest and an invisible hair-net. Instead of bobbing low to sniff portulaca and soldier-boy, I'd stride out over the footpath cracks; taking long steps, only occasionally looking back.

Perhaps. I wasn't sure. For Meg was coming tomorrow. She would need me. She'd hold my hand and we'd go for walks. But not that far from home.

I was prepared to show I was sympathetic; to squeeze her fingers and take the walks; to exchange the special glance that showed I shared the secret.

But Meg came back to the Gully and didn't want me. She might still be bleeding between the legs, but you'd never have known. She hid the smell, if there was one, under a snowstorm of carnation talc. She painted on a smile, and fastened the clasp of the Feather Shop necklet.

Meg was pretty again, as fetching as Miss Zena Dare. She was lucky enough to possess a skin of a tolerable thickness. Anything dirty could be washed away with a minimum of friction. Breakfast was kidneys on toast; last thing at night she did facial massage.

The butcher's son took Mother's hint and called. His hat hung on the peg in the passage, and the front room was scented with brilliantine. Meg sat at the piano and sang "Rose of My Heart". Mother served butterfly cakes for a snack. Father kept looking sulky—no one was good enough for Meg, according to him. Not even a regular supply of fillet and loin, for the price of hind knuckle and scrag-end, could persuade him to change his mind.

What Madame Mora made happen didn't mean a thing. Meg would have a tea-gown, and fold her table-napkins into the pyramid and the fan (but never the palm, the lily, the cactus) as Mrs Beeton explained. The butcher's son was charming. He scrubbed the blood from his fingers before he came to tea.

But his hand felt sweaty when you shook it, and standing beside her he looked like a boy. She was younger, but you wouldn't have thought so. "Not *quite* so much lip salve," suggested Mother. "It can make a girl look hard."

Her lips were reddest of all on the days we visited Rina. I went with her every weekend; I had a feeling she went other times, too.

We pushed up the slope and her ear-rings were bobbing. She wore her best. And there would be no one to see: only Miss de Mole, focusing between prayers; only Rina.

Burrs stuck to her skirt. There was cockspur and stinkweed to get through before we sighted the house.

Now cinerarias and marigolds ousted poppies and pansies. The dwarf leaned on his cut-down hoe and measured our approach.

Miss de Mole was still melancholy-nosed. Rina was brushing her hair and singing:

"I stand again in the North land,
But in silence and in shame;
Your grave is my only landmark,
And men have forgotten my name ...

Miss de Mole must be old—she had been in bed for years. But she didn't have a wrinkle; it was a child's face, queerly embalmed, that stared at us from the pillow. And her hair didn't have any grey. It was thick, and when Rina let it fall loose it hung all the way down to the carpet. But it was dead looking hair. It hung straight and stiff, and smelled of pimple cream.

Jesus was there in the room. Miss de Mole spoke to Him and He answered back. He told her not long now, that she was living close to the Border Land. Soon He would say "It is enough. Come home. I will give you rest and perfect peace." Miss de Mole dribbled a bit in gratitude, and Rina wiped up the spit.

Out on the landing she shrugged and said the old girl was on the decline. Ga-ga, almost. But life was bearable. Would we care to see her room?

She opened the door, and it was like fairyland. Everything sparkled. Love and Mercy's electroplating couldn't compete.

In between the sparkles there were toys: a rocking-horse that didn't lack a tail, a battalion of wooden soldiers. "They were Tommy's," said Rina proudly. And the sparkles belonged to the best things in the house—the silver epergne and the crystal lustres, the French clock and the ruby glass vase. "All mine," cried Rina, throwing out her arms. Diosma might be dotty but she shouldn't complain.

Anything Rina asked for she got—she had never had it so good.

What we saw was only the tip of the iceberg. More would come, oh yes. Dear Di was going to write out a will, and Rina would be featured as adopted daughter. Gladwish House would be hers. She'd wear silk petticoats and be *persona grata* wherever she chose.

Our visits were always the same.

Miss de Mole would praise God, and exhibit some new tribulation. Now she had whitlows on both hands and neuralgia in her head; now her Strong Helper had taken away her voice— she was dumb for several days.

Rina would sigh on the landing, and present us with new treasure-trove: an enamelled butterfly with garnet eyes and a modest sprinkling of sapphires on each wing; a pair of mechanical dolls—you turned a handle, and the cavalier and his lady linked hand to tread a clockwork minuet.

Meg stared, entranced. She was powdered and painted, with an eighteen-inch waist, but the grown-up world slipped away. She kicked off her shoes and lay beside Rina on the hearth-rug to cheer the toy soldiers into battle. They'd do jigsaw puzzles with their heads close together, and curl the wax doll's ringlets round their fingers. I was ashamed of them. Meg affected a little-girl lisp; Rina sucked her thumb. They were playing: it wasn't real. But I was frightened and ran to find Cuff.

He kept on being my friend. We walked in the garden to the trellis of vines. Now there were leaves, and grapes so small they were only bunches of dots. A caterpillar dropped on Cuff's cap, and he removed it to dislodge the pest. I saw he was bald as an egg. Where the edge of the cap had rested was a dent, resembling a hollow vein, circling his head.

Old Cuff talked the flavour of Rina's room away.

Who would have guessed that once, long ago—before the doilies and sewing threads claimed her—Miss Meek had been known as Gipsy, because of her eyes. Long and slanty and boot-polish black—hadn't I noticed? Oh yes, Gipsy Meek had been every lad's dream girl. Then ... And in winter when you cut dandelions for the cows, they were white with frost, and it hurt your hand to touch them. Remember, remember ... Aunt Ida Cuff had a muff made from musk-duck pelts. Uncle Maurice Cuff had a pet magpie, a friendly bird. Maggie used to love turning upside down on Uncle's knee, claws in the air, and going fast asleep.

Remember, remember ... And I walked home with Meg, and couldn't help it. My tongue forgot, and enquired of Miss Mott. Was she still Meg's friend, or just a cockroach—someone to be stamped on, who wasn't worth two pins?

Meg went stiff, but only for an instant. Then she smiled and swished at a fly. They were the worst things about summer coming, weren't they? She looked at the sky, and the trees covered in creeper, and the lilies that grew by the creek. She was smiling and her voice was sweet, but—oh, so puzzled.

"I don't know who you mean," she said. "Pixie Mott?—who's she?"

Miss Mott didn't exist. There was no Palm-house, either; not even a Botanic Gardens. A kidney might be served up on toast each morning, and Mother might intimate it to be only a matter of *when* (for the glasses of celebratory fizz, the twinkle-twinkle diamond cluster); but, really, there was no butcher's son—even though he stood at the piano, and trembled when he turned the page.

20

A Young Ladies' Mutual Improvement Society was formed to be twin to the Men's. A discussion took place in the Institute Hall on "Were ladies more courteous fifty years ago than at the present?", but Meg didn't go. Nor did she keep up her classes at the School of Design. Or attend Madame Clara Butt's recital at the Town Hall, or turn out for the Druids' Procession in Rundle Street, where the Victory Lodge did Caractacus appearing before Claudius, and the ancient rite of cutting the mistletoe was represented in a drag drawn by bullocks.

Meg concentrated on rites of her own. Now her world had shrunk small, and was bound by a hedge of prickly acacia. Most afternoons she set off for Gladwish House in elegant clothes. It was getting hot again, but she didn't care. Nothing could stop her going. She fixed her eyes on the sky and kept walking. Once, when I walked with her, a fly was on her lip but she didn't notice.

Though she looked all right. And ate every morsel of kidney, and nibbled the chops to the bone.

The butcher's son kept trying. He wrote a letter every day and sometimes the postage stamp was placed upside down on the top left hand corner of the envelope, which meant "I love you"; other times it went right way round, meaning "Goodbye for the present, dearest".

But Meg never read the letters. She put them behind the paper fan in the grate; posted them on to nobody. It seemed a pity that all those words should go to waste, so one day I stood in as reader. It was disappointing. He chopped up animals in an apron stained with blood, but as pen-pal his hands stayed lily-white. His letters were a let down, there wasn't a hint of passion.

You knew he cribbed from a guide to correspondence (court-ship and matrimonial), with his "Language fails to express how sedulously I have watched your every movement, how breath-lessly I have hung upon each word you have uttered".

No wonder Meg walked towards Rina and those afternoons of being a child.

At school the inspector came, and Mr Kitto was praised. For we knew that an elk was a large kind of deer, the size of a horse; a gentle creature, except when teased by the gadfly. That Galileo went blind through staring in telescopes. That rhubarb was introduced into England about the year 1810 by Mr Myatt, a gardener of Deptford.

My granma had grown rhubarb in her shoe; my uncle's name was on the obelisk. And I concentrated so much on my text-books that soon I'd know as much as Hilda Nutter. And I knew things the *Observer* told, too. How Queen Alexandra had even the Kohinoor diamond, but the jewel she valued most was her engagement-ring set with a beryl, an emerald, a ruby, a topaz, a jacinth, and an emerald, again (the initial letters of these stones spelling the pet name she gave her husband).

But there were things I would never understand.

Miss Rodda, a Salvationist, had a ring like the Queen's—hers spelled *Dearest*, but was spirited away. Miss Mott, a New Wom-an, could even better that, being wiped from existence, herself.

And some nights I couldn't bear it in the house. Her mouth kept opening and closing on "See, Love, I Bring the Flowers", while his Adam's apple flexed in readiness for "Down Among the Dead Men". But the Meg who sang so sweetly was a fake, and the butcher's son was being taken for a ride. I felt they were stuffed, like dolls—Mother, tapping the melody with her foot while she reached for another butterfly cake; Father, bunching his lips at the teacup, trying not to make a noise as he swal-lowed, when really he wanted to pull the bottle from the daisy bush and take deep gulps and fall on the grass while the stars swam overhead.

I couldn't stay there, just as stuffed as them. I went into the lane, where there were nettles and pools of shadow. Lizzie's house still stood empty; the gum-trees whispered dryly. Then two of the shadows started moving. They held hands and ran across the lane; they went through the briers into the wattle and daub hut. I'd seen them do it before. Only this time Teddy held Rina's hand rather than Meg's.

But he was engaged to Miss Beck.

And then they were married in the Cathedral, and the newspaper listed the presents. Bride to bridegroom: sovereign case; father to bride: cheque; mother: glassware ... Lucky Miss Beck, with an eight-day clock, a silver egg cruet and butter dish.

The newspaper told how they would honeymoon overseas. Teddy would take rapid sketches of Sydney Harbour scenery, and then tour New Zealand in quest of subjects for his palette; subsequently journeying to England by way of Capetown, in order to study the mist effects of Table Mountain.

The Saturday after they departed, Rina was happier than ever. She made Winnie bring us afternoon-tea, and she had the tablecloth changed because it was specked with iron-mould. When she had the house life would be different. First, she'd get rid of the Rays. She couldn't stand Winnie's face, and the way she peeped and pried. And who ever heard of a dwarf garden-er? Oh yes, when Rina had Gladwish House things would look up. She inclined to Eastern decoration: coolie servants and ta-ble-bells with emblem cobras for handles. When Diosma died they'd have them—her and Meg. Mulligatawny soup for break-fast; melon-flowers in the garden.

I finished my tea and they sent me away to Cuff. Today it would be toy theatre, and Meg could choose the play. Which did she prefer—*Beauty and the Beast* or *The Casket of Gloriana*?

I reached the end of the history book, and started once more from the front; revised the dawn of civilization, where the kings had crinkly hair and Cleopatra melted her pearl ear-ring in vinegar, so she might drink Mark Antony's health in costly draught.

That was all right, but I longed to get past the Crusades and Cromwell's ugly nose. At the back of the book, put in as an extra, was the best part of all. The explorers made bird-tracks in the sand, and skirted Mount Deception and Memory Cove.

I had more need of them, now, than ever. As well as Meg, there was Baby to worry about. Mr Kitto was whacking again. Baby walked home regularly with proof of Teacher's excesses on his bottom.

Mercy's charms had gone stale. And yet she looked just as good. "But the trouble is," said Love, talking more to herself than to me, "Teacher has a peculiar streak ..."

He liked them to call him that—Teacher; he liked Mercy best in the dress with the Puritan collar. But she drew the line. No, not on your life. He might beg, but she had to refuse. She wouldn't dress up as a child. Pinafore and ringlets, indeed!

More thrills were guaranteed by merely pacing infant room aisles: Mr Kitto ceased calling. Mercy didn't get the bound edition of the *Popular Educator* he'd promised. It would have been nice knowing things—What is amber? Where is the elephant found?—but not to worry. Monday and Friday were Ronald's nights; Te Aroha was still on the cards.

But Baby fell from favour, too. Love said she'd like to see Teacher frizzle in Hell. Mercy suggested consultation with the Chairman of the Board of Advice. Love shook her head. "And end up with Alfred being taken away; put in the Salvation Army Home for troublesome boys?"

So Baby suffered, and all I could do was pray. God had turned into a man, very tanned, crossing the desert on a camel.

Then it was another Saturday, and Meg and I were at Gladwish House.

Monday was exams and I was memorizing tables—troy weight, avoirdupois, square measure; and "Thirty days hath

September, April, June and November ..." when the door knocker sounded. Hardly anyone used it now. Rina had frightened most of Miss de Mole's callers away; there was even a scarcity of love-tokens through the post.

Meg and Rina stopped playing tiddlywinks, and I followed them on to the landing. Mr Kitto was climbing after Winnie up the stairs.

Doctor had told him, he said, how the poor invalid lingered on. Neither in this world nor that. He had come to pay his compliments before the end.

Rina's eyebrows drew together, but he didn't appear to notice. He was looking at her and licking his lips. Which was a bad sign, but Rina wasn't to know. She began dimpling again, and dismissed Winnie in a pretty voice.

"But of course," she murmured, "I will escort you." And contrived to show a fetching ankle in open-work stocking while she did so.

Teacher lived in the widow's house by the butcher's. The widow was Miss Meek's friend. She was always in the drapery; elbowing across baby lace and low embroidery to enumerate her lodger's virtues. Miss Meek rolled her gipsy eyes and passed on the compliments to Mother. Teacher was a paragon: the schoolroom was lucky to have him.

He pulled the boys' ears and whacked Baby Pettigrew and made the little girls cringe, but the widow-lady thought him a pet. He got cod's roe croquettes for breakfast; his lunch-time sandwiches were wrapped in vine leaves; he came home to something tasty for tea.

Teacher hit you if you talked in class, or rubbed out with your finger, or drew the Jonathan apple wrong. If you were poor and came to school without boots you must stand on the platform and be laughed at.

But the widow said Mr Kitto was lovely.

Each morning she brushed yesterday's scurf from his jacket, and coaxed it over his crooked shoulders. At night, while the beehive clock ticked, and her needle scaled the Jacob's ladder in his sock, she savoured the thought of him in the very next room—godlike, at the dining-room table, bestowing a storm of crosses on exercise books; or pondering some learned tome, adding to his inventory of curious facts.

Sometimes, over bed-time cocoa, Teacher confided to the widow that he yearned to travel abroad. Oh, if only he wasn't a schoolmaster, labouring for a pittance. It was well enough knowing capers to be the unopened flower-buds of a low creeping shrub growing wild in the South of France and upon the walls of Rome, Sienna, and Florence, but he longed to test the fact with his eyes.

Mr Kitto would sigh, and say it was all right for some—*viz* Teddy Teakle, venturing overseas on the proceeds of jam ... Miss Meek's eyes went soft with emotion. The widow had said how the poor young man was aquiver with despair as he'd cursed his lateral curvature. If it wasn't for that, he vowed, he could have attracted a bride in pocket.

Miss Meek told Mother how her friend had patted his spine, and said Now-now; that there were others worse off, and money didn't mean a thing. Why, at Gladwish House was Miss Diosma de Mole—rolling in it, but abed for ages, and apparently about to croak. Tee-hee, she said—and it was a tease—what a pity you're not down in her will.

And then the widow had told Miss Meek, who'd told Mother, that she'd blushed all over. She felt awful: vulgar: as if she'd spoken ill of the dead.

For her lodger hadn't answered a word. But sat still, like someone turned to stone, only his fingers moving—stroking his chin; then—somehow—pawing the air. He disapproved so much of her tone (and it was only a joke) that he'd risen and retired to bed. Like one in a dream. Hadn't even touched his cocoa.

Teacher came calling.

Miss de Mole quit dying to revive.

Colour crept into her cheeks and her puppy-dog eyes opened wide. She spoke again. Though she looked forward with pleasure to the home-call, and peace-perfect-peace for evermore, maybe it wasn't time yet.

Rina was summoned to shampoo her hair. Really, it was shockingly greasy; and why not try a different style?—the plaits twisted round, sort of a coronet.

And Winnie must hasten to the draper's and purchase a stock of nighties, and a bed-jacket that was all little loops.

The bureau needed dusting. She rather thought pineapple for dessert. And where was her large-print Bible?

Miss de Mole gripped the pencil between her teeth and composed a new acrostic:

L et not your heart be troubled—John 1:14.
E very perfect gift is from above—James 1:17.
O magnify the Lord with me—Psalm 24:3.

Leo was Teacher; the acrostic was for him. It looked like a labour of love.

But Rina, who'd been displaced as love object, didn't appear put out. Though she propped up the coronet with hair-pins and ushered in the Rays for resumption of Morning Prayers, she hardly seemed to notice things were changed.

Weekends meant parlour games and Gloriana's casket as well as Teacher's visits.

In any case, Rina saw Mr Kitto's coming differently to Miss de Mole.

On Saturdays and Sundays when the knocker sounded she nudged Meg slyly. By the time he'd reached the landing she combined dimples in the cheeks with a baby pout.

Mr Kitto lingered outside the sick-room and partook of a pinch.

Rina giggled as she resumed concentration on tiddlywinks. Safely claimed as doting admirer—merely another Lizzie, Diosma, Meg—Teacher might be dismissed.

The game went on. I kept score. Rina was winning comfortably.

22

I was older, for I had a birthday. I was Sagittarius, and that meant fire, and the turquoise was my stone. I got a copy of the *Girl's Own Annual*. It was best reading the Answers to Correspondents. Meg might have Rina, but I shared the Editor's advice. "Unhappy Scribe" should buck up, for though her verses lacked cadence "And the light of a star on the sun's faint path" was a promising line. "May-blossom" was warned that a furred tongue at morning was symptom of gastric disturbance; "Bashful Sixteen" shouldn't walk out with gentlemen after dark.

I got handkerchiefs and a pair of shoes, too.

The shoes were like a grown-up's, I couldn't walk in them. Father frowned and said they didn't suit, but Mother declared them perfect.

I was a big girl, nearly left school. Next birthday my hair would go up while my skirts went down. After that, who knew?

Mother started a story that was the same as all the old ones. But this time she substituted my name for Meg's.

Meg wasn't a heroine any more. She was done with, finished; off Mother's hands. For persistence had paid off. The butcher's son had repeated his question and finally Meg had succumbed. Now he could squeeze her waist and remove his jacket in her presence: they were engaged. Now there was only me to be made into a proper person who would lead a proper life.

"Leave the kid alone," said Father, but Mother kept talking. She was going to retrim my summer hat. Nothing looked as tawdry as faded rose-buds.

It wasn't true what she said. How I must get out more, mix, make a friend. Not Baby Pettigrew who was simple or Hilda

Nutter who was a swot. But a girl who combed her hair in front of the mirror and had a nice brother. A feminine girl, cheerful. A friend could work wonders; and sometimes vice versa. Thank goodness Meg had cast off that mannish Miss Mott.

It was a lie: I'd never lead a life like that. Safe in the Hills— next year, and all the years after—I would burrow in. Sneak into my hole in the earth like an ant. Go on reading the Editor's advice, and pull out the soursobs. The world wouldn't get me. Perhaps I'd have a cat, and could look in its mouth for hair-balls.

I told her. How I loved them so much I never wanted anything different. Her scones were that good; when the fruit-trees were in blossom the Gully resembled Heaven.

Mother laughed. Her face came awake. She looked the same as she did when Father was George.

"Don't be silly," she said. "Life's not like that. You can't stay a child for ever. And Pup and I aren't made of money. No, indeed, my girl. Birdies have to leave their nests. It's either wedding-bells or a job."

If I was sensible and cared about my appearance, of course they'd indulge me with extras. There was always spon for necklets and face cream; for classes in repoussé or a stint at something commercial. Nothing serious, mind. A blue-stocking scared them off.

Father looked troubled. I thought he was going to save me. But the flush on his face died down. He turned coward and began rubbing his leg. "Perhaps Thea could be taken on at the jam factory," was all he said.

"Never," cried Mother. "No, certainly not."

But there was the butter factory at Gumeracha. Or serving in a shop was permissible, as long as you chose something genteel.

I wanted to shout; to be an animal, and claw and bite.

I'd been foolish enough to think I had a choice: the Hills or learning?—this life, that? I'd never had one, but I hadn't known. The luxury of dilemma was for others.

I called her fart-arse under my breath. I hated them both. And God and all the explorers.

Surely they knew how I felt and were laughing to see me captured? But no. The evening went on just the same. It meant so little to them that Mother hummed while she tested the iron with spit, and Father made for the lavatory, whistling.

I decided to match them in nerve. Tomorrow was the start of exams. I would do as well as Hilda Nutter and not consider what came next.

The explorers didn't entirely desert me.

On the last day at school, after Mr Kitto's talk under the pepper-trees about taking our place in Society (the boys), and being the Mothers of Tomorrow (the girls), I went out the front with Hilda Nutter to collect my prize. We had tied for dux in the Certificate exam. I got one of the Lily series: *An Endless Chain* by "Pansy". Hilda's was one of Miss Yonge's.

Some of the girls who were leaving had tears in their eyes, but I didn't care a bit. Now, all that effort over and the ink pumiced off my fingers, I didn't feel a thing. I was sure I'd never feel anything again.

Not feeling was the best way; Meg was a good example. Her wedding-dress was nearly finished, but she didn't appear to give marriage a thought.

Perhaps it ran in the family: I could make time stand still, too. I lay in the grass and looked at the sky. The leaves of the fruit-trees covered bits up. The grass was dry and bleached; the apricots were ripe. It could have been any summer, any year. Not now, but then. And I thought of Granma and Uncle and Lizzie; and in the cemetery on the Terrace in Adelaide more dead lay under the same hot sun. The men of the Overland Telegraph Line; the Irish who requested your prayers.

In the grass were ants and beetles and snail-shells.

... It was funny how snails were still a pest in summer; how Father had to mix salt and soot in a bag. And each evening

pace the garden, walking windward of the flower-beds, beating
the bag with a stick. The dust flew out, causing every snail it
touched to die.

But more snails came. Sparrows and starlings nipped the
fruit, and several foxes had been sighted. Reynard was cele-
brating Christmas early. He'd paid more than one visit to the
Methodist Manse; on the last occasion breakfasting on duck.

Pests were everywhere. In the paddocks and lanes were in-
vaders come from abroad, so bold they approached the garden.
Cape dandelion and sweet scabious; wild turnip, whose other
name was Nancy; soursob and Salvation Jane.

Other detestabilities were dust, flies, mosquitoes. And the
black snakes that coiled on the road.

But the snake was nice. You were small: it was allowable to
be a child. You liked the snake. It was the same as the eel in
the picture-book from England. But Father jumped from the
buggy and hit with his stick ... Another day, then—when there
was a buggy—he said he had a surprise. You'd often said butterflies were your favourite things. He led you round to the front.
And the buggy lamps were thick with them—furry moths, all
squashed.

They ruined things. It was always the same—people were
just as much pests.

In the grass I captured time with my fingers. I laced them about
it; there was no escape. Stay still, I said, and it did. Time was
only the weaving ant or the ladybird whose house was on fire. I
was safe. And brave enough to outstare the sun, and not shiver
when the lightning struck.

For one day the sun went away. Suddenly the sky was dark.
Then it was pricked with dots. Rain fell in blobs that turned
to stones. It was hot; my neck was sticky. I smelled under the
arms, but ice, like barley-sugar lollies, dropped from the sky.
I lay on the grass and the hailstones hit me. There was lightning (some called it God's lasso). Thunder took hold of the sky

and shook it; the trees were streaming with rain.

"Come in, you little fool," shrilled Mother from the verandah. I jumped up, her voice made me. And time got free. I lost it. I could never find it in the garden again, no matter how hard I searched.

23

The Methodist Church held a Strawberry Fête. It was opened by the Mayoress, who was received by a guard of honour composed of young ladies dressed in white. Each lady carried a decorated wand, with which they formed an avenue, under which the Mayoress walked.

The sweet stall was bowered with red poppies and wheat; the work stall with pink poppies and fern. As well, there were produce, plain needlework, pot plant and handkerchief stalls.

For entertainment the Misses Beaver danced a ribbon dance—the Highland fling. Mr Rowley, the popular local singer rendered "Swallows", and as encore "Ye Spotted Snakes".

Meg assisted at the sweet stall. She didn't seem to care she had the chance of a free chew on stick-jaw: Mother intimated she should smile.

The minister's wife had arranged a procession of decorated go-carts. There were gasps when first prize went to Mercy Pettigrew's entry (and her not even a church member) that had the cart done with bluebells and, for occupant, Baby in his sailor suit.

But the new minister, who did the judging, was soft. He had the cheek to let in a party from the Home for Incurables. The lady at the pot plant stall shuddered behind the aspidistra, and said it shouldn't be allowed. It quite took the sunshine from the day. Some of them must have been making faces when the wind stopped blowing; the one in the Bath-chair didn't have legs.

Time pushed me on to betray Old Cuff. I smirked into my hanky just as gamely as the real grown-ups. I walked past the poor sufferers, careful not to stare.

Only Meg did that. Staring was bad taste—didn't she know they couldn't help it, but were smitten of God? Staring hurt their feelings, but Meg looked and looked. And, would you believe it, she even let the old one—worst of all, with bones more suitable to an elephant poking through her clothes, and rocking the pretend baby in her arms, and rolling her eyes to Heaven—Meg let her touch her face. And she gave her a bag of coconut ice. Mother moaned softly, and asked why she had to show us up. Why smile at the old rag-bag, but ignore the Mayoral party? And any other newly engaged would have made a point of flashing the ring.

Thank goodness for the refreshment tent, where you could get a cup of tea. Mother spooned in sugar and began to recover. Didn't the minister's wife look stupid?—really, the Riviera tunic skirt at her age.

This year's tent was doing bumper trade. As well as the strawberries there were scones—they made them on the premises in a portable kerosene stove.

But I couldn't eat for ever; we had to come out. And then there was Baby Pettigrew to dodge.

It wasn't fair. He insisted on following me about. Didn't he know I'd left school, and was done with childish things?

Oh dear. I felt ashamed when I remembered how I'd permitted Baby to be my friend. As for Mercy ... "Common as dirt," said Mother. "Take my advice, love, and keep away. Company tells. And I reckon you should start rubbing in cold cream at night. You can't take wrinkle precautions too soon."

I took my place in the fanciful parasol parade. I stood behind a girl they said went to Methodist Ladies' College in the city. She even turned round and smiled.

I blocked out the sun with my parasol and began marching.

As usual, it was a swindle. Mother had done wonders with wistaria, but the prize for best decorated went to Hilda Nutter's snow effect. Reverend called it original—well carried out: holly leaves all round, a robin perched on top.

"Piffle," said Mother. He only chose Hilda—the softy—because she had greasy hair and a problem skin.

Overseas, the *Observer* reported things happening: Miss Nightingale, Lady of Grace of St John of Jerusalem, was awarded the Order of Merit. In Sweden the Poet King died.

Across the border, in another state, there were grasshoppers on the train line from Bendigo to Melbourne. So many, that the wheels of the engine made a mush of the 'hoppers, and the rails were so slippery that the wheels that came next would not grip.

In Sydney you could purchase an instrument made of vulcanite which, placed to the eye, enabled you to see what went on behind your back.

I wished I had a Seebackroscope, or some similar optical curiosity.

At the Gully, from one point of view, nothing seemed to happen. You could hardly count the Strawberry Fête. Or the Improvement Societies' Social that terminated the season's meetings. Or the Bazaar to meet the cost of installing acetylene gas in the Baptist Church.

None of those events rated a mention in the *Observer*. Nor did the fact that Meg's wedding-dress hung, sheathed in tissue-paper, behind her bedroom door.

I was to be the bridesmaid. Now Mother had started off on my dress. The carpet in the front room was a danger zone; you couldn't go in barefoot, for you might tread on a pin.

Mother sang as she urged on her Busy Bee sewing-machine. Father put in the autumn-flowering plants and waged war on mealy bug, thrip, and red spider. Nothing happened.

But that was judging from one angle, only.

In the grass I'd almost trapped time. Sometimes, if I looked round quickly with a clear enough eye, I gained that other viewpoint.

If I concentrated hard on little things the life about me stopped being static.

... Mother's mouth gloating, satisfied, as she sliced ivory silk to fit the paper pattern's dimensions; Father rejoicing as he crushed the snail underfoot—while all the time the worm coiled close to the rose.

I didn't like what I saw. The facts revealed weren't comforting. Questions begged to be asked.

Did Meg really think she could marry him? Why was Mother making her do it?

Things were happening; an ending approached.

Even this year's *Observer* had one. Now we'd reached the Christmas supplement issue, and Mother had pinned up the full-page photo of "Great Pals" (two puppies, touching noses). Next Saturday's paper would usher in another year. This week's gift suggestions—all that exquisite perfumery, those dainty toilet novelties—would be consigned to the small print of the sale page. There'd be the surety of a new beginning, nicely familiar. "Ludo" of Goodwood would keep hoping, and advertise in the Matrimonial column for his plain middle-aged lady (R.C. preferred). The Scottish Hercules would return to the Hippodrome. Dr Williams would tell how hundreds saw her: helpless paralytic, carried through Sydney streets; how she was healthy and strong today, thanks to those celebrated pink pills.

At night, after I blew out the candle, I pulled the blankets about me. It was hot; I couldn't breath. Once, in the dark in summer, I'd felt safe. The night was so big I could lose myself in it: I'd kicked back the sheet and slept easily. But now I needed a second skin for protection. Sweating under best merino I made myself small. So the thing that came close couldn't get me.

Endings were terrible. You hardly ever reached one. The days seamed neatly together. Though the *Observer* had a different date—really, each year was the same. Most stories were all right, too; the brothers Grimm played fair, and let Snow-drop escape from her coffin. The spells were always broken, the beasts ran back into the wood. Jorindel touched the cage with his flower, and the bird turned into Jorinda: they went home and lived happily together. You started a new story content, knowing life went on for ever, after the old one's final full stop.

The hymns we sang in church guaranteed good times coming, too. There was always a shelter in time of storm; a green hill, a pearly gate. Jesus was the lily of the valley, the bright and morning star.

Mother rustled the newspaper and said wasn't it awful. You read over her shoulder. How the little girl fell into the fire and Doctor held no hope. Poor thing, she died—it must have hurt. You thought about it for a while, cried a bit, imagined it happening to you. But next day it didn't seem so bad; it would have been over quickly. It turned into a story. You stopped feeling the flames on your skin.

Always, there was hope. Gentle Jesus. Red sky at night. Counting the daisy's petals.

The pimple would clear up. Irish stew was horrid, but you liked the dumplings that came with it. The early Christians, assured Reverend, bid dying friends Good night, so sure were they of their awakening on Resurrection morn.

But Meg. What would happen to her? She wouldn't wake up. Not even when the butcher's son played Prince Charming and gave her kisses. I saw them by the gate. But she stood stiff while she let him do it. She was a walking talking doll. Nodding her head in the right places; smiling into the mirror; only coming to life as she climbed the stairs to Rina's room.

24

On Christmas Eve the main street of the town was decorated with evergreens. The school band assembled outside the Institute Hall to entertain with selections and carols.

Christmas morning came in with a sharp frost, an unusual event. The watermelons turned black overnight, but the raspberry canes remained a sight to be seen.

The day passed off quietly. After turkey dinner there were sports on the field below the Baptist Church. Last year I'd won the Patriotic Handicap, which was three-legged, with Baby; this time I didn't have a partner. I watched him toe the finishing line with Hilda Nutter.

We went to the butcher's house for tea. There was a smell of meat in the passage, and a telescopic table in Australian walnut. Next month Meg would be moving in. It was a far cry from Queen Anne and Marseilles tiles, but her fiancé was fond of his mum.

This year there wasn't a school picnic. Mr Kitto was occupied with other matters.

Now the holidays had come he visited Gladwish House daily. Rina had caught him massaging Diosma's toes.

People were beginning to talk. Teacher had forsaken little girls, and the mothers didn't like him. He'd fallen from favour with his landlady, too. The widow told Miss Meek that he wasn't company any more. She kept brushing the scurf from his collar, but he hardly spared her a word. He didn't confide. It was unnatural—all that cloistering in a dying lady's bedroom.

The widow had made Christmas dinner as nice as she could. There'd been floating flower-bowls on the table, and fringed paper round the turkey legs; Miss Meek had attended as special guest (wouldn't it be good if she and Teacher ...?). There'd been lucky charms in the pudding, and though poor Gipsy got the old maid's bell, Teacher spooned up the wedding-ring.

"Tee-hee" said the widow, kicking her friend under the table. Mr Kitto blushed—it looked promising. But after he'd gulped down his tea he was off like a flash. It was too bad of him.

Rina took over the story; she told Meg next day. How he'd raced to Gladwish House and sat down to a duplicate dinner. Teacher and the invalid together. *Tête-à-tête* in the sick-room.

Christmas Day saw Diosma looking perky. She wore satin ribbon round each plait and her bedjacket with the pom-pom tie. On the bedside table, gift-wrapped, was the love-token for Leo that her teeth had worked in secret: a silk bookmark embroidered with a lighthouse. She smiled between mouthfuls, even though Mr Kitto refused seconds.

Rina spoke of Miss de Mole and Teacher as we climbed Gladwish House's tower. She'd never taken us there before. The narrow stairway cut us off from the rest of the house. Our voices dropped to whispers: we went where no one had gone for years.

The tower afforded an excellent view. Hills were massed together as far as the eye could reach. Lake Alexandrina and the Gulf of St Vincent were reduced to thin blue lines. Fern Gully lay below us, a story-book village. Further afield was the fertile valley of Piccadilly, patched with market-gardens.

The Hills were full of secrets. Even up the tower you couldn't see them—the things that were hidden away. Waterfalls, a baronial vice-regal summer residence, a railway line to Melbourne. In the earth, under the tangled hedges of sweet-brier, were copper, gold, and bismuth; diamonds were even rumoured.

From so high up the view was perfect. Niggling little things—flies buzzing in the lavatory, curl-leaf on the peach-tree—didn't exist. Rina smiled down benevolently, as if the Hills were hers.

Meg's voice ruined it. The words sounded hard and bright:

Mother's voice when she surfaced from dreaming.

"What if she marries him?" asked Meg.

I felt embarrassed. How could she ask, and acknowledge what everyone but Rina seemed to know?—that Miss de Mole would keep living long enough to become Mrs Kitto. A new will would be made, just as Rina predicted, but Teacher would be the only beneficiary.

Rina kept smiling. Then I saw that she was laughing. She hugged her body and laughed without making a noise. She held out her hand and Meg took it. They pressed close to the edge of the parapet.

The hills in the distance were a foreign land. Life must be different there.

Rina had Meg in her arms. She was kissing her like a man.

Sometimes, on one of the scorching summer afternoons there came over the parched hillsides, which then looked bare and arid, the same violet shade or reddish-purple that was to be seen on the cliffs of Arabia.

True, true. The history book said so. The heat prostrated the men, and even the bullocks were sunstruck. For a length of time the chief subsistence of the party was the eggs of the Mallee pheasant.

There were no birds, only a constant sighing of leaves. The gum-trees sounded sad. Deep in the earth their roots coiled and twisted. I knew I had lost Meg for ever. "Jump?" Rina asked. "Shall we do it?"

I wanted it to happen. I would run along the Gully Road, my screams making scissor-cuts at the air. "Poor girl," they'd say, lowering their voices. "Her sister died, you know."

But now Meg was laughing, not Rina. The ending hadn't come; I was cheated of my final full stop.

Meg took off her engagement-ring, and threw it into the sky. For an instant it was up there with Jack's beanstalk and the woman who cleaned the moon.

Her finger getting free called for commemoration. We went

back to Rina's room, and the bell that summoned Winnie rang imperiously.

But Winnie didn't come. Rina stamped her foot at reality. First thing she'd do when she was Mistress would be to send the Rays to the workhouse.

She led us down to the kitchen. Cook had made a Christmas cake that had six eggs and four tablespoons of brandy; chopped nuts and glacé cherries, mixed peel and a teaspoon of spice. Its almond icing was shaggy with desiccated coconut; there was a holly-sprig and a crêpe-paper frill.

As we reached the kitchen Mr Kitto was coming out. He smirked when he saw us. Rina flourished her tongue at his lateral curve.

But her tongue couldn't match the greater smirk that filled the kitchen. It enveloped us as we entered the room, and the Rays surveyed us. The quality of its malevolence was compounded by the scorn in Winnie's eyes, the complexity of Cook's gurgles, the dwarf's off-hand belch.

Rina raised her voice. "Winnie," she repeated. "I rang, but you didn't come ..."

The dwarf belched again—louder. He seized Pearl Biddle and began exploring her neckline.

Pearl screamed and waggled her stump. It was evident that the Rays had been tippling.

Winnie minced forward, and dropped Rina a curtsy. Her voice quivered in mock servility: "You rang, Miss? Oh dear, whatever was I thinking of that I didn't answer?"

The Rays sniggered on cue.

"Cake, Miss?" said Winnie. "Oh dear, what a pity ..." Now she had straightened up. Her lip stuck out, her hands were on her hips. Her voice went loud and started to wobble. "The fact is, Miss, the cake is all eaten up. By us. Me and Cook and Pearl and Gardener. In celebration. What, Miss?—oh, don't say you didn't know. Oh dear, they must be keeping it for a surprise ... Go on, Gardener, you tell her."

The dwarf abandoned Pearl Biddle to join us, grinning.

Why was he born so tiny? Why was his beard like that?—one side black, the other grey. He hated us—Rina in particular. He had veins on his nose. It was a lumpy nose. Big, for such a small man.

Cook was shaking like a jelly, the gurgles were coming that fast. Pearl Biddle adjusted her bosom. Winnie picked her nails with the bread knife.

The dwarf was telling us the greatest love story in the world. Rose-bud slept behind the thorn hedge for a hundred years, till the Prince came through and kissed her. Rina covered her ears. The story was wrong: Diosma was betrothed to Gentle Jesus; Teacher was happiest tickling little girls. "No, no," Rina cried. She wouldn't believe. Meg fondled her ringless finger and started to hum. It was boring—I'd known all along. "Be quiet," cried Rina. "I won't listen." But the dwarf kept talking. It would be Rina who'd end up in the Destitute Asylum, not the Rays. After the wedding the new master would put her out. How sorry the Rays would be.

Rina was sobbing. She was a loony again. Only an infant, but Teacher didn't like her. The dwarf tapped his head. Winnie said for God's sake to get her out. Rina was fighting, jerking her arms. The dwarf smiled as Winnie hit her face. She went limp, but there was no Lizzie to carry her to bed and dose her with soothing syrups.

Old Cuff was by the trellis. He let me sit beside him, and didn't expect me to talk.

After a while I felt like telling him. How everything was terrible and would never come right. Only Miss de Mole would be happy, with Teacher standing in for Jesus.

"Wrong," said Cuff, and caught the sun with his mirror. Sunshine was cast about the garden, broken into little patches.

Dear Madam, according to Cuff, was unhappier than anyone; worse off than she'd ever been.

Once, when Madam was being tried in the furnace of afflic-
tion, her face had a look of excitement. It stared at you from
the pillow—shiny, exultant. Life might be awful, but Jesus kept
her company. There was no place for guilt or doubt: she greeted
each day with "Thy will be done" and "Even so, Father".

But now, when Teacher left the sick-room, Diosma lost her
perk. She kept pondering her Bible and plotting acrostics with
fervent pencil, but her eyes were dead.

Poor Miss de Mole. Once she'd been strong. And so ridiculous that she resembled a caricature. Clever people couldn't
explain her away; they had to talk of her with a laugh in their
voice.

If you were brave enough, and gave up enough, you usually
got your first wish. You weren't allowed a second. Diosma had
missed out on sainthood by yearning to be ordinary. Now she
was only small beer, not worth much more than Pearl Biddle.
The best thing by far, said Cuff, would be for the silver cord that
held her earthbound to break, that she might again approach
angel heights.

25

That night I couldn't sleep. It was hotter than ever but I huddled under a blanket. I tried to think of Cuff and what he'd said about being brave and getting your wish. But the night pressed close. I curled small, but could never escape it.

Morning came. At last there was white light, and it was allowable to sleep—nothing would come at morning. As the false darkness swallowed me up I heard rustling—something moving in the passage. But it was all right: only someone off to the lav.

And then there were birds all round. I woke in a jungle. I kept my eyes shut, so the leaves wouldn't wither or the voices—piping, bell-like, shrilly ruffled—fade away. But the sun started tickling, and there was the smell of bacon from the kitchen. I opened my eyes to the bedroom: hair-tidy, handkerchief, yesterday's bloomers. The birds kept up their din, but they were only magpies and spoggies. Their voices remained exotic, but I stopped bothering to listen.

Breakfast was the same as usual. Mother ate one-handed as she kept her place on small print. Her skimming finger caught up on other people's lives. It was easy to feel a winner with so many hard luck stories to choose from.

Sometimes, when there was a tragedy ("Head dressmaker at well-known drapery emporium takes tumble down the lift well") her finger turned gentle and soothed the anguish away. A mystery was the best, though. Then—no names mentioned, tastefully anonymous ("Mutilated body recovered from the Torrens", "Twin skeletons found in the sandhills ... bones crumbly but complete")—it was permissible for your finger to skip jauntily and a smile to hover. This morning there was a choice one—"Oh, Pup, did you ever?" Strange reappearance ... Alfred Boldner, believed eaten by sharks, had lately been sighted in Melbourne. Mrs Boldner had refunded the insurance.

Her mouth muddled the words with egg yolk, and Father sighed. A stranger's reverse was a tonic for Mother—one less dash of reality that could get her. But Father shrank from the impingement of a world where something happened. All he wanted was the reassurance of a long stretch of meaningless days. If life was nothing, how could you be blamed for being nothing yourself? He hunched over his plate, and tried to drown the testimony of Mr Boldner's try at freedom as he slurped down tea. He longed for the garden where pansy faces didn't accuse; for the almanac's predictabilities, the pick-me-up of the morning's first sight of Meg.

But Meg didn't come. Mother read on: past Horticultural Hints for January and this week's News from The Empire. Meg was usually late, but not as late as this. You couldn't keep a kidney warm for ever.

Father was sent to give her a call. I started to know ... Yesterday was real, not this. Standing at the top of the tower, the two of them clinging together. And, before that, under the fruit-trees, their bodies flattening the grass. Father called again and then he went into her room.

Meg had gone. But in the story there was always an envelope propped at an angle. You opened it to find the reason why. Your scream was muffled; you said "No daughter of mine", and struck her name from family annals.

"Meg, Meg," cried Mother. The bedspread was tucked in neatly under the pillows; there was a smell of carnation powder. Tissue-paper littered the floor.

She had put on her wedding-dress and rustled away. There was only one place she would be.

We ran down the Gully Road. The morning extended before us, everything was marked with its freshness.

We chased her as fast as we could, but I knew she was too far ahead. Meg had got free. Of Mother's tongue and a world where Bowden was common and dreaming ended with cramps in a palm-house. The butcher's son would never catch her now.

Mother had a brooch that was a map of Australia. And a Busy Bee sewing-machine and a copper fern bowl. She had a Bible full of neglected words and bridesmaid's fern. None of it guaranteed safety. I was frightened, but I wanted to giggle. It was farcical: the rule that you had to rub in hand cream, and how you must kiss her cheek for you might smudge the lip salve ... and where was she now?

We crossed the bridge and reached the top of the slope. Gladwish House stood where it was meant to. Everything was the same; more and more I wanted to laugh. Mother had longed to come here. Properly invited, she'd have worn her dress with the pleats and her hat with the ribbon flowers. Now, come unbidden, her hair was a disgrace and her dress the one for wash-day.

The garden was as trim as ever; its floral patches sprouted gallantly from the sunburnt earth. Mother looked the other way as we passed the fishpond.

We crossed the gravel like bit-players making their entrance. Cuff stood on the verandah in his night-shirt, mirroring our approach. "I knew someone would come," he said. "But it's too late—she's dead."

But he didn't mean Meg. It was Miss de Mole who lay at the top of the stairs with her night-dress rumpled, and her skinny legs sticking out. Her legs had hairs on them, silky and black; her toe-nails were yellow and old.

Miss de Mole shouldn't be there. She was meant to die in bed. Miss de Mole couldn't walk or move or do anything. Year after year she had languished between the sheets, imprisoned by the stationary days. Lying there she'd started to live. Teeth gripping pencil, eyes fixed on large-print Bible she'd announced herself Christian and larger than life. I'd seen her sad nose and helpless hands, I'd wondered about bed-pans and times of the month; I'd known how much it plagued her—but, really, I'd never connected Miss de Mole with a body. Now she sprawled on the landing, immoderately possessed of one. Mother knelt to adjust her nightie.

A miracle had taken place at Gladwish House. Miss de Mole rose from bed and walked to meet Jesus.

Cuff upstaged Mother in starting a story.

Yesterday, Meg had talked Rina to recovery. When we left she'd been smiling and believing again—what the Rays said wasn't true; Diosma would never ditch her. But that night Rina had been summoned to the sick-room, where her fall from favour was confirmed. Winnie, who'd been there too, said she'd taken it well. It was only later that things began happening.

We sat on the stairs. The temporal part of Miss de Mole still lay there, but Cuff's voice dismissed it. Even Meg's flight in ivory silk stopped being something we must arrest. It was important to find her, but Rina's story needed telling first.

I felt as if I'd been there—one of the Rays. Up in the attics: Cook gurgling on as she confronted that dream dinner dished up by angel fingers; the dwarf snuggling closer to Pearl Biddle's stump; Winnie, under cover of darkness, treating her sour mouth to a reckless grin; Cuff hooped on his side, nose meeting knee ... Then sounds: glass shattering, doors slamming, Rina's voice raised loud. And the Rays turning petrified, tipsy courage deserting them. Only Old Cuff hooping from bed towards danger.

"She was rampaging," he said. "She was smashing things up. Master Tommy's toys and the ruby glass vase. Her hair flying, a wild look in her eye. Not a stitch to cover her body."

Father nodded, engrossed; Mother made saucer eyes.

All the time she was singing away. An unlikely choice, sentimental. Cuff caught mention of roses and lands of snow, before the ending was rendered *crescendo*:

"'Tis a tale that is truer and older
Than any the sages tell.
I loved you in life too little,
I love you in death too well."

Rina was still singing and smashing, regardless of Cuff, when Miss de Mole came loping in.

Sight of Diosma enraged her. Rina ran forward, flaunting the mole on her belly at the virginal bride-elect.

Jesus made a miracle, but Miss de Mole wasn't used to being upright. Overwhelmed by Rina's advance she fell to the floor. A little of the Divine grace lingered. She had strength to crawl to the landing while Cuff aimed his hoop at the loony. By the time Rina was subdued and he was able to reach dear Madam's side all her tribulations were over.

And it was morning. And Meg stood at the foot of the stairs.

Cuff said her name and it wasn't a story, pleasantly entertaining, any more. Mother began to cry. Father gripped the Ray of Sunshine's shoulder. "Where is she now?" he asked.

But, for Cuff, reality ended with Miss de Mole's passing. Meg had swept up the stairs in ivory silk and spirited Rina away. "Gone," said Cuff. "Look for yourself—the house is empty."

For Cuff's cowardly fellow-Rays had departed, too. They marched from the attics in orderly crocodile, bridged Diosma's remains, and continued down the stairs. The Rays of Sunshine were respectable: what had passed at Gladwish House that night did not bear thinking on. Their protector taken, who knew what might come next?

Cuff thought that Gardener and Pearl Biddle were off to join Fenton's Circus. The dwarf had heard of an opening for a miniature Goliath, and, with practice, Pearl fancied she'd prove efficient on the aerial trapeze (surely swinging one-handed should draw the crowds?). Cook would gurgle on over other people's saucepans; Winnie was pinning her hopes on the Matrimonial columns ("Refined Protestant lady, blue eyes, seeks respectable gentleman, abstainer").

Mother and Father stirred impatiently. The stairs were hard, and they had little interest in the Rays' prospects. Meg's whereabouts were on their minds.

Father descended to ponder the natural landscape. Mother searched her hanky for a dry spot.

She was transfixed in mid-snivel by Father's reappearance. He bounded up the stairs as well as his bad leg allowed. "Hope!" he cried. "There's bits of her wedding-dress all over the garden."

He led us outside again, to the dwarf's prize bed of roses. Sure enough, snared on sharp-tooth thorns were tags of silk. Father wove his way between the bushes, whooping as he found another snippet. Mother followed gamely.

Cuff and I retreated to the trellis. "Now they're past the cinerarias and marigolds," I told him. "Now they've reached the stone dog and Venus."

Mother and Father's route was familiar. They retraced the path to the creek we'd so lately taken ourselves.

Cuff was silent. He resembled some out-of-shape Old Testament prophet, hunched beside the grapes in his night-shirt. I liked him better when he wore his cap—without it, his head was fragile. I wondered how old he was; I hoped he wouldn't die too soon. I thought of Meg and Miss de Mole. Mother and Father had looked happy, playing tag to the creek. You might have suspected there to be hope; that Meg was still somewhere to be hunted out and trapped into another try at life. Mother and Father's pursuit denied that death existed; Diosma's body on the stairs didn't count ... Dear Miss de Mole. She had escaped as well—from a robber-bridegroom and Sleeping Beauty's couch—with the bonus of a miracle thrown in.

Cuff was thinking of Miss de Mole, too. He spoke of her reverently—of her goodness, reclining there day after day; of the countless invalid pen-pals who'd gained from her example; of her kindness to the Rays.

I swung my legs and sucked on a sour grape. Suddenly I felt sick of things. Old Diosma, life in general ... even the grape didn't have much bite. I was tired of being charitable. Spread out on the landing, hairy-legged and comprehensible, Miss de Mole had become a bore. I liked my saints mysterious. "Perhaps" and "maybe" were comforting words. I swallowed the grape and turned optimist. Mother and Father were right: you had to keep smiling and believing in something. Perhaps Meg was still running. Maybe I'd visit her in Melbourne.

Cuff concentrated on his mirror. I looked into it and he stared back quizzically. "Thea," he said, "I will tell you something I'd never tell anyone else."

Miss de Mole slipped from easy patronage to become someone I'd never known. Cuff might have been Teacher, peeling another layer from the man on the oilcloth chart, he so completely swept away my illusions.

All those years Miss de Mole had lain in bed, smitten with a mysterious ailment—and Cuff was saying that all those years, instead, she might have been walking about. Breathing in the mild Hills' air, charting the fishpond's ripples, directing the pencil with her fingers and not her teeth. For, all that time, Diosma had merely been normal. Her afflictions in the main were imaginary, and nothing to do with Jesus. As last de Mole she'd wilfully abdicated from life to turn herself into a legend.

What a fraud, what a sham. Cuff nodded his head in agreement when I said she had a nerve. I kicked the trellis and didn't know what to think. One part of me disbelieved him—he was making it up. But why should he? Cuff had loved Miss de Mole; he'd known her better than anyone.

Though I felt indignant at her deception, grudgingly, I had to admire her. Tricking the doctors and outwitting the Rays couldn't have been easy.

I believed, but: "Why did she do it?" I asked.

For answer, Cuff conjured up another Diosma. An English rose, only slightly cankered; a superior Gipsy Meek. Someone nice enough, but unmemorable: bookish—regularly conning her Bible; splurging, and thrilling to the wild rhythms of "Hiawatha" and the hexameters of "Evangeline"; in dress habitually favouring shades of duller hue, that she might creep through life unnoticed.

"She could have stayed like that," said Cuff. "She might have married and told of baby's first tooth."

But one day Diosma stopped creeping, ceased being prudent and started living. She willed her body into something grotesque; swaddled it in the gauds of High Fantasy. She took direction of her days, and chose Jesus for phantom helpmate, and inclined her body to stillness. Now and then she was deviant and paced the sick-room in secret. Cuff stood at the keyhole and spied her.

Rina came, and Jesus wasn't all-sufficient. Fleshly pleasures suddenly seemed nice. Miss de Mole fretted, and longed for her old content. But, even as she commenced declining, Satan blocked her escape. He led Mr Kitto behind the acacia hedge: Miss de Mole was smitten.

"Imagine," said Cuff, "her anguish. He wanted her as she seemingly was—an invalid, on the down-grade. She hankered to have done with pretence."

It was an act of God when Rina went on the rampage. Diosma might be soulful, but the de Mole tidy-mindedness lingered. It hurt to hear all that glassware being shattered, not to mention the routing of Tommy's toy soldiers. On reflex she rose. Her problems were solved when Rina charged.

Cuff contorted his neck and met my eyes outside the mirror. "Do you see now," he asked, "how she lived a grand life? Think of what she achieved by cheating. Think kindly of her; think kindly of Meg."

He didn't need to say any more. I sat beside him by the trellis; the vines frilled about us. It was turning into a lovely day, not too hot. The bees were bumbling already.

Cuff took my hand. His fingers were cool and dry. He looked ridiculous, still in his night-shirt.

Meg was an explorer. She was somewhere with Burke and Wills and all the others who'd braved the interior.

26

They found her by the creek. She lay beside Rina beneath a
lemon-tree twined with creeper. Meg and Rina lay together in a
leafy room. The world outside was shut away. Under the tree it
was cool and shady. The grass there was green; in other places
it was bleached by the sun.

Rina was wrapped in a Chinese shawl. She wore rings on her
fingers and an Albert watch-chain as ankle bracelet. Fastened
to the shawl was a cameo and a stick-pin.

Meg's wedding-dress was dirty and torn. It was only fit for
the rag-bag.

She had rustled away. Perhaps God whispered in her ear and
revealed that Rina needed her; perhaps her visit was arranged,
formally, the day before. Really, it didn't matter how Meg came
to be at Gladwish House; why she'd erred in taste, and dressed
unsuitably for a morning call. She'd come and Rina had been
waiting. They joined hands and ran through the roses and took
the path to the creek.

The creek had dried up. Instead of water you confronted
pebbles. And twigs and fallen leaves. The creek was no good—it
didn't offer escape ... and who wished to emulate Lady de Mole
with a dip in the pond?—she'd overshadow them, ever-lasting-
ly, because of departing by way of it first. It would have been
nice to frequent Menzies' Hotel where they served American
soda drinks and you sat in the Egyptian Lounge to wait for commercial travellers ... but Melbourne was too far away—Rina
couldn't think how they'd get there. They sank down under one
of the trees. It was a little green room. They held hands and Meg
laughed because it was good—being with her favourite person,
the worry gone from her head. For a while they were children.

Rina said Tinker-tailor up and down her buttons. Rina had no buttons, so Meg counted her moles. Rina said Shall we do it? and Meg nodded. But it was hard to think how; it was pleasant just sitting. Rina sang her song again and then they laughed about Diosma—hadn't she looked a sight on the landing? Diosma wasn't that bad, though—Rina felt a bit sorry she'd bumped her so hard, and there was a crack when her head hit the floor. Lizzie fell, too. By the creek—but not here. Further along, near the Baptist Church. That day they were gathering herbs ... And Meg said Couldn't we eat something? It happened like that in the *Observer*. You ate cyanide, you ate oleander. Rina had green fingers; she knew about plants. Lizzie had told her things, too. She said You must never pick these. These ones are poison.

Meg and Rina died. Father was friends with the doctor, and he turned it into an accident. Meg and Rina were girl friends who ate wild lilies for a joke. They were put in the cemetery with Granma and Lizzie and the others. Diosma was there, too, but because of being a de Mole her grave had a sad cypress and an iron fence. You went through a gate that was hard to open and there were angels and Lady de Mole and Sir Harold and Tommy.

Meg had glass tulips; their stems ended in knitting-needle points that went into a vase filled with dirt. Rina had a big twisted shell and something strange and stony, pitted and frilled—Father said it was coral, though it wasn't a pretty colour, only grey. No one knew who put the shell and the piece of coral there.

She was dead, and it made a difference. Mother and Father changed. They seemed to reverse their roles. Now it was she who kept silent and spent her day in the garden; it was he who told the stories. They were mostly Do you remembers; mostly to do with Meg. Remembering, Father could look her in the eye. He wiped the make-up from her face and it was as if there'd never been a Teddy or a Rina.

Father gave Mother a book called *The Cloud of Witness*. It had a cream cloth cover embossed with gold. Inside was a picture

of Jesus with a lantern, and on every page a selection of con-
soling thoughts—several for each day of the year. Mother read
her book religiously. At the back there was a page where you
entered departeds' names. Mother wrote in Meg's and, opposite, a poem about weeping not, nor letting the air with sighs
be troubled. The pen she used had a nib that made the words
look Gothic.

Mother took her own advice. After a while she hardly cried.
People said How brave. She did the flowers at church, and went
on the committee for improving the Recreation Ground.

And Father stopped hiding bottles in the daisy bush. And
he rattled the money in his pocket and said Why not buy some
more land? He'd plant more apple-trees, and: What about a
cow, what about a horse and buggy? We used to have one—do
you remember?

It was funny. I hadn't believed they'd be able to bear it; I'd
thought their lives wouldn't go on. But it was as if a burden had
rolled away. Meg had been something they could never live up
to; their efforts to make her over into one of themselves had
led to that morning by the creek. Father would have killed anyone who hurt her—how could he kill himself? Besides, only
Mother had the right to call him guilty; only he had the right to
judge her. If you didn't acknowledge something how could you
be sure it existed? Time passed, and Father was able to speak of
her and keep smiling; Mother contemplated a rose arbour for
her grave.

Their lives had always been shamingly little, but with Meg
gone littleness was easy to accept. The shame went away.
Bowden became a place you could allowably recall. Father sat
at the table in his shirt-sleeves and smoked Yankee Doodle, and
it was all right to have a glass of beer. Mother called him George
all the time now. I saw him kiss her in the passage.

Other things happened at the Gully.

Cuff stopped being a Ray and went to the Home for

Incurables. Miss de Mole's will said Gladwish House should go to the Methodist Church, and Miss Meek told Mother that it would soon be a Rest Home for convalescents.

Teacher departed, too.

After Diosma's death his spirits were naturally low. Then he started getting the letters: poison pen. The widow found one in the bin. It was dreadful what the letter said. Of course it wasn't true—but who'd have thought it? Each morning one was in the letter-box; each morning Teacher left most of his egg. And he had the trembles and was grinding his teeth. She told Gipsy who wondered if it was safe to have him in the house—she'd always suspected him of maniac's eye. The next one she found was all little bits. Crook-back was trying to fox her. But the glue-pot was handy; and being sticky-fingered proved worthwhile: simply disgusting ... she hadn't known you could do it so many ways. "It is my duty," the widow told Gipsy, "to warn the mothers. A kiddie could be ruined for life." Not long after that Teacher ceased venturing out. The staring must have got on his nerves; and that time butcher brandished the chopper. He didn't bother with meals. She heard him pacing at night—and mumbling, and sometimes a laugh (what if he lost control?). She told Gipsy he'd have to go. Next day she had the words ready—just as soon as he should appear. But he didn't. No, not even by morning-tea. She took him a cup on a tray—now he was going she nearly felt sorry. After all, none of it was probably true. It was shocking how rumour spread. But she needn't have bothered with refreshments—and there was date cake and a paper doily—for her lodger had fled. He must have left by way of the window. Taken his fibre suitcase. Under cloak of night. He was never seen in Fern Gully again.

It was Love who wrote the letters. I saw the poison pen and the bottle of Blue Swan ink.

I was a visitor at Pettigrews' again; I was Baby's friend. But things weren't quite as they'd been. The perfect moment when

I'd sipped restorative wine and felt bees in my head could never be repeated. Love and Mercy still petted me but there was a stiffness behind the easy surface smiles, a wariness in their eyes. Though Love's spell as correspondent was a secret I shared, they kept mum about more routine matters.

The gentleman in sewing-machines wasn't mentioned. Or Ronald who'd promised Te Aroha.

You'd have thought (the episode of Teacher excepted) Love and Mercy to have been merely blushing maidens, perhaps wiser virgins than most, the spoils of their glory boxes—Wertheim three-thousand stitcher, tray-cloth and photo frame and cosy, all those assorted crystal sparkles—spread about them.

On reacquaintance, Love and Mercy were a disappointment. They seemed respectable. Love left off her dragon-fly pin and blood-red mouth. Her elegance had a hint of the sartorial; she didn't wear pearls by day. And you'd never have suspected Mercy of a penchant for monkey fur and satin. It had been lovely when she'd been common. Now you hardly saw any flesh; she crossed her legs at the ankle and didn't offer a taste of her tongue.

For, Meg dutifully mourned to the grave, the butcher's son had transferred his affections. Now Mother paid full price for fillet and loin. It was Mercy who ate kidney each morning.

And Love made regular trips to Cudlee Creek. She'd met a gentleman, a horticulturist, who was also a champion ploughman (having secured twelve first and four second prizes in the course of seventeen contests). He overwhelmed her. She did the same to him. What had begun as casual acquaintance blossomed into a love-match. He called a new variety of plum after her (not Black Diamond or Grand Duke but the Love plum). They were to be wed at the end of the month.

And things were looking up for Baby. Teacher departed, he was decidedly improved. No whackings to fear, Baby was eager to learn. Hilda Nutter had been giving him special coaching. It seemed a sure thing he'd be promoted from the infants'. His head didn't appear so big or his eyes so sleepy. When Mercy moved into the butcher's house Alfred would be going too.

Meg died. The days passed and it turned into a different year. But it was still summer. You put cucumber peel on your forehead and worried about bushfires. The apricots were finished, but the cherries were at their prime. You couldn't stop eating; your lips were always purple.

February would come: I'd take the morning coach to the city and become a Christian lady's country boarder. It would be funny to go to the high school.

But at weekends there'd be the Hills.

We'd knock the almonds and sit on the verandah and shell them. The Easter daisies, that always bloomed early, would open. March: sudden storms, and the garden choked with the scent of shattered roses. After a storm you smelled flowers everywhere.

COPYRIGHT

This print edition published in collaboration with Brio Books, an imprint of Booktopia Group Ltd

Level 6, 1A Homebush Bay Drive · Rhodes NSW 2138 · Australia

Print ISBN: 9781761280726

briobooks.com.au

MIX
Paper from responsible sources
FSC® C008194
FSC
www.fsc.org

The paper in this book is FSC® certified. FSC® promotes environmentally responsible, socially beneficial and economically viable management of the world's forests.